THE HOUSE

THE HOUSE

Leonie Hall

CHIVERS

British Library Cataloguing in Publication Data available

This Large Print edition published by AudioGO Ltd, Bath, 2013.
Published by arrangement with the Author

U.K. Hardcover   ISBN   978 1 4713 6135 7
U.K. Softcover   ISBN   978 1 4713 6136 4

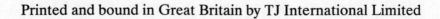

Printed and bound in Great Britain by TJ International Limited

CHAPTER ONE

Leaning against the back of the chair Amy McKenzie raised one arm and held her hand out palm down. She examined it, pleased with its steadiness. She had never considered herself the nervous type or to be easily frightened, but Max had left her jumping at shadows, subject to dreams that woke her shaking and bathed in perspiration.

Max! Two years of marriage to Max with his unreasoning tempers. His possessiveness, his demanding she account for every minute of her day. She recalled the sting of his slap when they'd reached their home the day he'd called to pick her up from school and found her talking to one of her male colleagues. He'd begun casually at first, asking who the teacher was, why she was spending time with him. Building into a temper. By the time he turned the car into their driveway he'd worked himself into a rage that frightened her. The slap had knocked her against the garage wall and sent her staggering sideways. From then on the assaults became more frequent and more violent, until finally unable to endure any more she'd fled. Still she'd not been safe. Max had waited outside the school each afternoon demanding her return. Sometimes begging, at times threatening. The telephone calls were the same. She bought an answering machine, but still was not free of him, the messages he left made her shudder. Then she would see him late at night, sitting in his car outside her flat. Watching.

Desperate, she sought an intervention order and the police warned Max of the penalties for stalking. Then the threats began in earnest. Letters made of words cut from newspapers. Telephone calls with no-one at the other end of the line. The day she found a dead cat on her doorstep, its throat cut, was the culmination of months of worry and fear, and she collapsed in a weeping, soggy heap and casting aside all pretence of independence, moved in with married friends and for the first time in over a year felt safe.

*   *   *

There was no visible sign of Max, but slowly Amy again began to feel certain he was still around. Somewhere. She found herself again tensing up, waiting for his game of cat and mouse to recommence.

'Go!' Her friends Sally and Greg had urged her, watching the colour fading from her face and seeing tension evident in the lines of her body. 'Get right away where Max will never find you.' Amy took their advice. She applied for teaching positions in various States and felt fortunate when her application for Bingurra

High was approved, and she'd moved from Brisbane in the tropical climes of Queensland, down south to the small country town in central Victoria. She resumed her single name and became Amy McKenzie once more.

*   *   *

It had been a short courtship. Amy had met Max at a social evening held to raise money for charity, wondering when she could decently leave without seeming rude. She'd noticed him standing by himself near the windows. He'd caught her look and smiled, his handsome features creasing into charming wrinkles about his light blue eyes. Unthinkingly Amy had returned the smile and Max had walked over to where she stood, drink in hand.

'You look about as thrilled as I feel,' Max offered.

'Is it that obvious?' Amy blushed slightly.

'Sort of.' His eyes danced with amusement. 'How do you come to be here if it's not too bold a question?'

'Oh I bought a ticket thinking that'd be it, but then decided I may as well come and see what was going on. What about you?'

'Much the same I'm afraid.' He shrugged. 'My name is Max. Max Harrelson,' he introduced himself. 'And you are?'

'Oh, I'm pleased to meet you Mr. Harrelson. I'm Amy McKenzie.'

3

'Mrs? Miss? Ms?'

'None of the above. I prefer Amy McKenzie.'

'Well Amy McKenzie, I'm pleased to meet you as well, and please call me Max. I'm not used to being referred to as Mr. Harrelson.' He smiled and Amy laughed.

Two nights later Max telephoned Amy and invited her to dinner. From then on their relationship progressed and three months later Max proposed and Amy accepted the diamond ring he slipped onto her finger. The marriage was less than a week old when the violence began. At first it was criticism of her dress, her hair, his demand that she be always within his sight. Bit by bit it escalated until the day he hit her. It was a back handed blow that caught her just below her cheekbone. Instantly Max was contrite, begging her forgiveness and promising never to repeat the performance, but it happened again and then again.

CHAPTER TWO

Amy switched off the motor and let her ancient green Mazda coast along the gravel road. She brought the car to a halt in front of the last house where the road finished in a dead end. For a long moment she sat behind the steering wheel looking dubiously at the house and its unkempt surrounds.

There was little in the way of rental housing in the Bingurra area. She'd looked at two other properties in town but neither suited her. One was far too close to the small but busy main street and the other, despite its sorry condition, was too far above the modest rental she could afford to pay. Not to mention the variety of damage both places had sustained. There were holes punched in several walls of one house and a large chunk of flooring missing from the kitchen in the other. This house was the third and last on the list the Real Estate agent had given to her.

This doesn't look too promising either. She tapped her fingers on the steering wheel. The house she now looked at seemed to be in dire need of much care and attention despite the warm comfort of its red bricks. Wooden window frames had long ago lost any hint as to their original colour and were now just oblong pieces of splintering grey wood. A narrow space of weed riddled dirt separated the edge of warped verandah boards from the sagging picket fence.

Amy could see little of the house surrounds other than two enormous willow trees growing where the ground at one side of the building sloped downwards to a small creek bed. Straggling wire between the willows suggested where the boundary lay. Vacant land overgrown with grass, stretched between the upside of the house and its nearest neighbour with a row of trees defining the border. However despite its derelict appearance an air of quiet seemed to hold promise of the anonymity and solitude she so badly sought.

'Okay, let's have a good look and hope this is the right place for me. Fingers crossed,' she muttered as she climbed from the car and made her way to the gap in the picket fence where once had existed a front gate, the only remains now being a pair of rusted hinges dangling from a leaning gate post. She stepped onto the dirt coated path and scuffing a sneaker clad foot across the accumulated grime of years, she detected a tessellated path of red and beige tiles set in diamond shapes leading from the gateway to the verandah. *Been nice once.*

Careful of where she placed her feet, she mounted the rickety verandah boards. Something dark flickering close to the corner of the house caught her attention. Changing course she turned her steps to the side and was in time to glimpse two people disappearing around the far end of the cottage. A man and a woman, both clad in black. The woman's coat reached to just above her ankles and a small brimmed hat tilted at an angle perched on grey hair. The man was bareheaded and walked half a step behind his companion.

'Hello?' Amy called. She hesitated then hurried after them. She rounded the corner, her lips already half parted in a smile, but found no sign of anyone. 'Drat! Where'd they go?' she asked out loud frowning as she looked about her. 'Hello?' she called again but there was neither answer from, nor sight, of the couple. 'Hello there,' she tried again, raising her voice. Still nothing but the rustling of leaves and the warble of a magpie somewhere in the trees. She looked about her, her forehead wrinkled.

There was nowhere anyone could hide, and why would anyone want to hide from her anyway? The yard was bare but for an empty garage minus its doors. A small shed, held closed by a padlock rusted with years of disuse, was visible from where she stood. She could see no other place of concealment. Next she turned her attention to the house and gave the rear door a couple of sharp tugs confirming it was securely locked and looked at the autumn leaves gathered in a thick drift against the bottom of the wire door. It was obvious no-one had entered through there in a very long time. Wherever the couple had disappeared to they'd moved pretty smartly.

With a shrug she returned to the front of the building and fishing a key from her pocket, unlocked the heavy front door. Eyeing the dragon shaped iron knocker with approval she pushed against the warped wood and entered the house.

She stood at the top end of the passageway.

The place smelled musty and her nose brought to her attention the scent of mouse droppings, along with the more pungent aroma of cat urine that wafted upwards through the floorboards. Wallpaper, ancient and discoloured buckled from the walls, and a narrow length of carpet running towards a half open doorway further along, felt heavy with dust beneath her feet. Her movements disturbed the dust causing her to sneeze. Shaking out her handkerchief she wiped her nose then kept the handkerchief in place, using it to help lessen the smell as she continued her exploration. Two doors on her left opened off the passageway. The first room, running parallel to the verandah, showed Amy a rectangular room, bare but for a small fireplace tiled in green and with a rusty grate standing in one corner. The walls were a discoloured yellow that she thought could once have been cream. The room directly behind possessed a similar corner fireplace tiled this time in dark red and backing onto the corresponding fireplace in the front room. The walls here were the same dismal shade as its neighbour but showed patches where once pictures had hung. At the end of the passage Amy pushed at the door, its top half panelled with coloured glass. She found herself in a large kitchen. Crossing the dusty floor she fished another key from her pocket and inserted it in the lock of the back door.

The effort taken to turn the key told her that no-one could possibly have entered this way recently. She left the door open allowing fresh air to circulate and dispel some of the musty odour within. A further glance around showed her a door to one side of the kitchen, a peek inside showed her a small room she thought would have been used as a storage area. She moved to the centre of the kitchen and despite the dirt and dust, liked the feel of it. Small windows either side of the brick fireplace shed light and an ancient iron stove sat below the wide chimney. Its hobs and hearth spoke to her of gently singing kettles, and bright flames to sit and dream into on cold evenings. Of toast and hot cocoa at hand and slippered feet warm on the oven shelf.

The sun shining through the skylight above made a yellow pool about her feet while she further took in the sturdy sink beneath a wide window that gave her a clear view of the back yard.

So far so good, except for the pong. She closed and relocked the back door and with a sigh and a smile walked back along the passage, wrinkling her nose and fishing out her handkerchief as the acrid smell again caught in her nostrils. The room corresponding with the one on the opposite side of the passage was her next stop. 'Nothing much here,' she decided. It was a plain room painted the same boring colour as the others with another

9

fireplace and one window that looked out along the side of the house where she had recently hurried by trying to catch up with the man and woman in black. A faint frown again creased her forehead as she recalled the speed with which the couple had disappeared. She shrugged dismissing the puzzling thought and went on to inspect the final room.

It was a good sized room. French doors in heavy iron frames opened on to the front verandah. She studied the frames and thought they seemed out of character with the rest of the house. A fireplace took centre position on the side wall. The room felt cool, but a quick peek at the sky showed Amy the French doors faced east and had lost the early morning sun. It would, she thought, make an ideal spot for breakfast on bright winter mornings. She could imagine a small table by the doors, the sunlight through the glass warming her, and soft breezes wafting in on hot days when she could have the doors open. *If they opened.* She would be sure to check on that. She decided she liked the place despite its neglect. She walked through the house once more, slowly this time, with notebook and pencil in hand and a critical eye gauging needed repairs.

Her inspection finished, Amy locked the front door, gave the dragon shaped knocker a brief pat and climbed back into her car. She drove into town, past the sign welcoming people to Bingurra and trying to ignore the niggling worry that the couple she'd seen earlier could possibly have also been potential tenants and beaten her to town. She frowned then shook her head. *People that age would hardly be interested in such a dilapidated place, especially one situated on the edge of town as well. So why would they be there in the first place? Also it's very odd how they disappeared so quickly.* Still puzzling over the mysterious couple she parked the car beneath the shade of a gum tree at the end of the main street and walked along the footpath where shade trees lined each side of the road.

Tom Floyd, one of Bingurra's two Real Estate Agents peered across the paper he was reading and shifted his feet from his desk top. 'Back again.' He smiled, creasing his moon face and adding an extra chin to the two already there.

'Yes.' Amy nodded. 'I'll take the house,' she added fishing in her bag for the keys. 'If . . . if no-one else has beaten me to it.'

'No danger of that love,' Floyd laughed showing a gold tooth to one side of his mouth.

'Oh.' Amy gave a small sigh of relief and wondered again about the couple in black. 'Ah, then there's no one else interested in the house? No one at all?'

'Not a soul, darl. It's all yours. Why? Have you come across someone that might be interested?' The third chin reappeared.

'No . . . no,' her words stumbled unable to

mention the couple in black, afraid she'd be laughed at if she said how quickly they had disappeared. 'I just wondered, you know.' She offered a self-deprecating smile.

'Well then if you'll sign these papers, you can put those keys right back in your bag. You'll have your work cut out cleaning up out there though. Got any ideas of how you'll manage? I can give you the name of a couple of people that might be willing to help out.'

'Thanks, I'll keep that in mind,' Amy replied, knowing full well she couldn't afford help of any sort unless it was free, and that didn't seem likely.

She departed the estate agent's office gently jingling the keys to the house she had just leased for twelve months. She looked with approval along the wide and dusty main street of the small township and felt a sense of the serenity she'd sought for so long, and was beginning to think would never find, steal over her.

A visit to the hardware store for much needed cleaning implements was next on her list then a trip to the town's only supermarket for a few provisions to take back to the house. Next week she would take up her teaching position at Bingurra High and her new life would begin. Until then she would devote her time to house cleaning.

CHAPTER THREE

'You must be the new teacher.' Amy turned from the desk where she'd carefully stacked her books and looked at the girl who had spoken.

'Yes,' she smiled. 'I'm Amy McKenzie.' She extended a hand.

'Glad to meet you Amy McKenzie.' The girl's grip was firm. 'I'm Elisabeth Jane Belling. Libby to my friends,' she laughed, 'and I hope that will include you.'

'Thanks.' Amy liked the look of Libby Belling with her fair curly hair and her open countenance.

'Nervous?'

'A little,' Amy said. 'What's it like here?'

'Pretty good, actually. More laid back than a big city school. Everyone mingles here, both in and out of school. It can be a bit of a hassle at times though if you've got some irate parent after you because they don't think you treated little Tommy right.' She pulled her eyebrows together then broke into a wide smile. 'It's not often anything like that happens though, so don't worry about it.'

'I see,' Amy grinned, 'thanks for the tip.'

'The bell's due to go soon,' Libby glanced at her watch. 'What say we meet for lunch in the cafeteria?

'Suits me, I'll see you then.' Amy watched Libby leave the room just as the bell rang and she settled herself to begin her day.

*   *   *

A sharp cracking sound startled Amy into wakefulness. Her heart pounding, it was several seconds before she realised where she was. With a sigh of relief she left the shabby but comfortable armchair and crossed the room to shut and lock the French doors. 'I thought I'd secured you,' she said as she took hold of the heavy frames now lying back against the wall. It had taken time and effort to get the doors working properly again. She'd scraped encrusted dirt from the frames, oiled the hinges and marvelled at the weight of the old key. She had polished the glass in the doors, feeling smug satisfaction when they glistened in the sunlight and threw patches of warm yellow sunshine into the room.

She glanced through the open doors and noted quite a strong breeze had sprung up and most probably forcing the doors open. 'I'll make sure of you this time,' she said, double checking that the doors were properly closed and the key securely turned. She returned to her chair and with a soft grunt bent to pick up the papers lying on the floor by its side and made her way to the kitchen to brew a pot of coffee. She would, she decided, finish the remaining few papers at the now well scrubbed kitchen table. The hard wooden chair would act as encouragement to remain awake.

It was close to midnight when Amy, easing her back with a long stretch, pushed her pile of finished work to the far side of the table and glanced around the room with an air of satisfaction. It was a month since she'd moved into the house and three weeks since she had commenced her teaching position at Bingurra High School at the beginning of the new term.

She left her chair and rinsed her cup under the tap before making her way to her bedroom, shivering in the cold air, comforted at the thought of the hot water bottle nestling between the sheets, for the night was cold. Winter was well into its stride and the grey days turned into cold nights, making her glad of the thick rug she had spread across the foot of her bed.

Moonlight shone white on the verandah of the house and turned the glass of the French doors into sheets of glittering crystal. Voices, soft at first, but growing stronger, penetrated Amy's sleep and she saw in her dreams the couple in black she'd encountered the day she had first looked at the house.

CHAPTER FOUR

'Hi. Mind if I sit here?'

Stifling a twinge of irritation at the interruption, Amy lifted her head and looked up at the speaker. Seated at a corner table in the staff dining room her back to the wall, she'd been intent on a history text concerning Julius Caesar, trying to ensure she would be at least one step ahead of her class at their next lesson.

'Help yourself.' She indicated the chairs around the table, as the tall figure lowered his tray to the table top and seated himself opposite her.

'I'm Matt Armstrong,' he said, glancing up at her in between transferring a plate of sandwiches and cup of coffee from his tray to the table. 'You must be Amy McKenzie.' He held out a hand and despite her initial irritation she felt her stomach flip like a pancake at his smile as she accepted his greeting and extended her hand in return.

'I thought I'd met everyone by now.' She closed her book, keeping one finger between the pages.

'It's my first day back,' he said. 'My mother died recently and there were a few things I had to attend to that kept me longer than I'd anticipated.' He smiled, his clear hazel eyes

16

watching her. 'Sid Dacre said you'd be joining us after the holidays. How're you finding things?'

'I'm sorry. Yes. Uh, good.' She tried to answer everything at once, shaking her head as she heard herself and feeling mean for her previous spurt of irritation. 'Let me begin again,' she said. 'I'm sorry about your mother, and yes I think I'll like it here, it all seems to be settling fairly well. Mr. Dacre . . .'

'This looks cosy, mind if I join in?' Libby Belling didn't bother waiting for a reply but sat herself down at the table's end and grinned at the others before dipping her face to her mug of black tea.

'Libby! How goes it?' Matt leaned back in his chair and smiled at the latest addition to the table.

'Good thanks Matt. Everything all right with you?' Her green eyes showed concern. Libby Belling with her snub nosed, green eyed freckled face and tousled blonde hair, was a complete contrast to Amy's olive skin, dark eyes and long wiry dark curls that insisted on escaping no matter how securely she tied them back.

'Did I hear you mention "Broad Acres" she said, using the irreverent nickname most called the head of Bingurra High behind his back.

Amy gave a light laugh and said, 'I was just going to say that he'd been a good help with getting me settled in here.'

17

'Give him his due, he's not a bad old stick,' Libby said. 'Are you quite comfortable at the house?' Her eyes turned towards Matt as she spoke, a slight hitch of one eyebrow gaining his attention. 'Amy lives in your direction, Matt. She's taken the old Tunney place.'

'Have you now?' Matt smiled again, showing an almost perfect set of teeth except for one slightly crooked, to one side of his mouth. Amy considered it saved him from nauseous uniformity. 'It's pretty quiet being at that end of the road. Not too lonely for you, I hope?'

'Not at all,' she said firmly. 'I like peace and quiet. It suits me fine.'

*   *   *

It was the small hours of the morning when stumbling out of bed her toes curling away from contact with the cold floor, Amy fumbled her way into the front room. She blinked against the sudden glare as her fingers made contact with the light switch and turned it on. The French doors stood open, bumping gently against the wall and letting an icy wind stream into the room.

The sound of someone calling out had disturbed her sleep. A woman's voice. Calling, sounding worried. She hitched at her pyjamas with one hand, then gripped the edges of the French doors and peered out into the night. She could see nothing in the pitch black. *No one's there, Amy. It must be the keening of the wind whistling through the doors. Next I'll be hearing banshees. Ugh!* This was the second time the doors had opened. She would have to get the lock seen to. It had seemed secure when she'd checked before going to bed, the same as the last time she'd found them open. She would have it looked at, just to make sure.

'Damn nuisance,' she mumbled, 'it's too cold for this sort of lark.' Irritably she closed and re-locked the doors then shoved the armchair up against them for added security, and crept shivering back into her bed.

*   *   *

It was Saturday and dressed in jeans and an old shirt Amy carefully placed a bucket of hot soapy water on the bottom shelf in the small room that opened off the kitchen. Until now she had ignored this room, leaving it until she had the rest of the house arranged to her satisfaction. Today, she decided, was the day to give it a thorough scouring. She intended to store her accumulation of odds and ends in here. Handy but unobtrusive.

She glanced at the round-faced clock on the mantle piece. Time was getting away from her. Libby and Matt were coming over to help roll out a piece of carpet and set up a desk in the middle room behind the kitchen, which meant the boxes still stored in there would have to be moved in here, but not before she had given the room a thorough clean.

Amy's friendship with Libby Belling was becoming as solid as though they'd known each other all their lives. Even her acquaintance with Matt Armstrong was progressing gently and steadily into comfortable comradeship. They were content to share a mutual liking and pleasingly, various outside interests. That is, if Amy could disregard the buzzing in her stomach each time Matt looked at her. Matt had once been engaged, Libby had informed her, his fiancée tragically killed in a road accident.

Ridiculous, she'd scolded herself. She had no right to feelings of this nature, and besides, she was definitely NOT interested in another relationship. No sir!

She had barely escaped a horrendous marriage from a man who terrified her. It was hopeless anyway. Matt had so tragically lost the love of his life and he definitely was not looking for a relationship.

Wearily she hooked an errant curl back in place and dipped her scrubbing brush into the hot water. She'd not been sleeping well this last week. She had got out of bed on several occasions thinking she heard raised voices and more than once had discovered the French doors open yet again. She'd return to her bed and fall back into a restless sleep to wake in the morning tired and unable to recall the dreams that had troubled her. She had not had the French doors seen to either. Too lethargic to make the effort she had simply placed the heavy armchair back in front of them and left it there.

Shelves finally cleaned to her satisfaction, Amy knelt ready to scrub the floor. Hesitating before she plunged her scrubbing brush into the soapy water, she surveyed the dry and cracked linoleum. She pursed her lips, suddenly deciding she would prefer a floor of bare boards. She began pulling at the brittle covering and found it came up in easy chunks which she tossed on to a growing pile of rubble outside the back door.

Almost finished and sneezing with the dust her efforts had caused to float around her, Amy bent to remove a scrap of paper jammed half beneath the chipped and cracked skirting board. Tugging the resistant paper free she straightened up, holding her back with one hand while she examined her find held in the other. It was a photograph. Old and yellowed, it was hard to distinguish properly in the dim light. She carried it to the kitchen, peering closely at it in the sun pouring through the skylight.

It was a picture of a couple, standing stiffly to attention. They were clad severely in black and looked sternly towards the camera. The woman's coat was ankle length, her hat tilted over one eyebrow. Her companion, in a dark suit, was bareheaded. Frowning she placed the picture on the table, her finger tapping gently on its surface as she studied it.

The sound of a motor coming along the side of the house wrested her attention from the photograph and she tossed it in one of the drawers in the big old-fashioned kitchen dresser before going to greet her visitors.

Standing at her back door Amy watched as Matt unfolded his length from behind the steering wheel of a shabby grey truck, and looking, she thought smothering an incipient grin, not unlike a grasshopper. A red haired man, a stranger to Amy, got out of the passenger side, allowing Libby to tumble out after him.

We're here.' Libby waved to Amy as she stepped across puddles, and by the simple process of holding the sleeve of the red-haired man's jumper, brought him with her. 'Amy, this is Jim Casey,' she said, introducing her companion. 'He's captain of the local footy team.'

'Hello.' Amy shook the hand of the man, liking his affable grin and laid back air and wondered if captaining a football team was his sole occupation.

'Thank you for your help,' Amy said smiling. 'I guess you got roped in willing or not.' She gave him a sympathetic look.

'It's all fine,' Jim replied, 'I didn't mind in the least. These two would be totally useless

22

without my guiding hand.' He laughed at Libby's cry of 'Wretch.'

'Hoi!' The call drew their attention to Matt standing at the rear of the truck its tail gate now lowered.

'Right-oh,' Jim answered for all and they crossed the yard to the waiting man.

'Here, you girls should be able to manage this rug between you. Jim and I will wrestle with the desk.' Matt pointed to the rolled mat wedged between the desk and the side of the vehicle.

Amy and Libby exchanged grins that said they really didn't want to wait around to see, or hear, the effort involved in getting the desk down and inside the house in one piece. It was a wide and cumbersome looking piece of furniture, and Amy wondered how they'd managed to get it into the utility in the first place.

'Do you think just the two of you can get it down without doing damage to either yourselves or the desk?' She laughed up at them. Matt and Libby had generously offered to collect the desk from a second hand shop in Willoughby when Amy had mentioned the cost of having it delivered and had obviously decided the football captain's assistance would not go astray.

'Good question,' Matt replied. We had to have help getting it up on to the floor of the truck at the store.' He frowned and rubbed

23

one finger across his forehead.

'Come on then Libby.' Amy grabbed the nearest end of the rolled rug and pulled, Libby caught hold of the far end as it slid towards her, and they proceeded inside to unroll the carpet on the floor before the desk arrived, toted by its puffing and red-faced porters.

With much heaving and groaning the men manoeuvred the desk around awkward corners. Matt was the only casualty when he jammed two fingers between desk edge and doorjamb, and rendered some colourful vocabulary into the dust-mote filled air.

Satisfied with their progress, Amy darted back into the kitchen to check on lunch, and placed the bread in its foil wrappings in the oven to warm.

Replete with soup and warm bread everyone sat back chatting while they sipped coffee. Conversation was relaxed now the hard work had been done and it was time for conviviality.

'Oh wait.' Amy left her chair and retrieved the photograph from the dresser drawer. 'Do any of you know anything about this?' She waved the snapshot in the air.

'Show me.' Libby reached out and took hold of the piece of paper. 'Can't say I do off-hand.' She frowned. 'It's pretty old, where did you get it?'

'I found it not long before you arrived. I was cleaning out that room,' she pointed to the

24

small side room, 'and found this stuck under the linoleum.'

'Do you know them?' Libby passed the photograph across the table to Jim's waiting hand.

With Matt craning his neck to see over Jim's shoulder both men examined the picture. 'Means nothing to me,' Matt confessed. 'Do you recognise them?' he asked seeing Jim's gaze fastened on the photograph.

'Ummm . . . they seem to ring a bell somewhere,' Jim finally supplied an answer, 'but I just can't put my finger on it. You found it under the lino in that room?' He looked at Amy and saw her nod. 'Perhaps they lived here once . . . it could be . . . it could just be the Tunneys. I wonder,' he mused half to himself.

'Tunneys. Of course,' Libby cried. 'This place used to belong to people of that name. I'll bet that's who it is, just get an eyeful of the clobber they're wearing, it's so old fashioned.' No one seemed to notice Amy's sudden silence.

*　　　*　　　*

'Hello Amy, did you wish to see me?' Sid Dacre, headmaster of Bingurra High smiled as Amy approached him in the school yard where he occasionally strolled during lunch time, getting fresh air and watching the goings on between pupils and the teacher on duty.

'Yes.' Amy hesitated then said, 'You've lived in Bingurra a long time and I wondered if you could be of some help identifying the people in this photograph.'

'Let's see.' He took the proffered piece of paper and studied it, tilting it toward the sun a small frown creased his forehead. 'Hmm, where did you find it?' he asked readjusting his spectacles to peer over their tops at Amy.

'In one of the rooms of my house. I found it when I pulled the linoleum up while I was cleaning.' She watched his face for an answer. 'Do you know them?'

'It looks very much like the Tunney's,' Dacre replied, staring back down at the photograph.

'The Tunney's?' Amy felt her stomach begin to curl. 'Are you sure?'

'Pretty sure. That used to be their home you know. Are you feeling alright, Amy?' Her face had lost colour.

'No . . . no, I'm fine, really.' She made an effort to shake off the sudden feeling of unease. 'I . . . it's just I haven't been getting much sleep lately. The French doors in the front room, they keep coming open and bang against the walls, especially at night.' She rubbed her arms to indicate the coldness of the night air.

'Having trouble with the doors are you?' The head master asked.

'Yes.' She gave a rueful shrug.

'Would you like me to take a look at them?' he offered. 'It's no bother,' he added seeing her about to protest.

'Well if you're sure,' Amy accepted the offer gratefully.

*   *   *

Half an hour after arriving home Amy saw Sid Dacre park his car in front of her house and she opened her front door to welcome him.

'I've brought some tools with me,' the headmaster said indicating the bag he held in one hand. Sid stepped into the room not waiting for a reply, and moving the restraining armchair to one side crouched down to peer at the lock. He twisted and turned the key, opened and closed the doors several times and finally stood still, scratching behind one ear with a forefinger. 'Can't see anything wrong with them.' He turned to Amy. 'They should lock easily enough.' He frowned, watching the worry lines crease Amy's forehead. He knew nothing of her background. He simply saw a young and attractive woman who looked rather anxious. 'Probably a truck,' he said.

'A truck?' she echoed blankly.

'Yes. We get a lot of heavy transport trucks coming through Bingurra at night.'

'But not along here,' she protested. 'It's a dead end road.'

'It's an old house and the vibrations

probably shake the house and loosen the doors.' He smiled reassuringly at her. 'This whole area was well mined in the old days. There are tunnels all over the area and they'd carry the reverberations through to here quite easily and loosen the doors.' He teetered on his toes then rested back on the flat of his feet as he re-appraised the doors. 'Pride and joy of old Tunney, those doors,' he said. 'Bought them at an auction over at Willoughby, and brought them home tied to the roof of his old car. Then he fitted them in this room. Used to fancy himself being able to walk out onto his verandah without having to use the front door. I remember hearing my father talk of it.' Sid rocked back on his heels. 'They were a bit reclusive, I think.'

'Will you stay for a cup of coffee?' Amy asked. 'It seems the least I can offer after the trouble you've gone to.'

'Thank you Amy, but no,' Sid said with a shake of his head. 'I'd best get back. I have to take young Peter to footy training and the wife wants another garden bed dug along the side of the house. 'You know what they say about no rest for the wicked don't you?' They laughed together and Amy ushered him out the door.

*　　　*　　　*

Amy folded the ironing board with sharp

28

movements and returned it to its place in her newly tidied storage room. Wryly she reflected that no matter what events took place in the world, be they of great or small moment, the mundane things in life still insisted on being coped with. She had slept little last night, tossing in her bed, turning Sid Dacre's words over and over in her mind. Accepting and rejecting in turn his identification of the people in the photograph. Doubting her memory. Afraid to confirm it.

*   *   *

The broad light of day failed to deliver the consolation of a sensible solution to her problem. She could swear, well almost, that thc couple in the photograph were the same people she'd seen rounding the corner of the house the day of her first inspection. She took the photograph from its place in the drawer of her kitchen dresser and sat by the fire while she studied the picture yet again. At a guess, she would say it was taken some time during the nineteen-twenties and the couple appeared to be middle-aged then. Rapid calculation told her that now, approximately seventy years later on . . . She shook her head. It was impossible. She found she was shivering and picked up a log from the basket on the hearth, ready to toss it into the already glowing fire and almost dropped it again, startled by rapping at her back door.

'Matt,' Amy said, relief and pleasure in her expression as Matt's large frame filled the doorway. 'Come in. Sit down. Coffee?' She was garbling words at him, pulling out a chair from the table for him to sit, diving to place the kettle closer to the centre of the stove.

'Amy,' he greeted her. He placed a hand on the back of the chair Amy pulled out for him but remained standing, one hip propped against the table. 'I wondered if you'd like to have lunch with me?' he asked amiably. 'I thought you might fancy a bite to eat at the 'Bill 'n' Coo.' Afterwards, I'll have a look at that sagging corner in there.' His nod indicated the room they had furnished with the rug and desk.

'Sounds great,' Amy didn't hesitate. Any distraction was more than welcome at present, and if she was enjoying Matt's company that little bit more of late, it could all be put down to the fact that they had come to know each other better

The Bill 'n' Coo, had once been the 'Classic Cafe' one of two cafes in Bingurra's main street. The advent of an up-market bakery and adjacent coffee shop saw a severe dwindling of patronage and the Classic Café closed its doors. Now, recently taken over by a more enterprising couple it was redecorated and converted into a B.Y.O. restaurant by W&P. Dove.

'I don't believe it,' Amy stifled a groan and then giggled when she read the names printed above the entrance.

'Sad, isn't it?' Matt grinned at her reaction. 'I think you'll soon forgive the Doves when you try their food.' He ushered her inside the café.

Amy gazed about her. The place was clean and warm inside and she soon discovered the food lived up to Matt's recommendation.

'Are you satisfied that you have everything put in place now?' Matt pushed his empty plate to one side and leaned back against his chair.

'It's all coming together quite nicely, thanks.' Amy smiled at him.

'You're settling in then? Think you'll stay and sort out the country bumpkins?' he teased.

'I think I'll settle without too much trouble at all, and I wouldn't say there was anything country bumpkin-ish about the place at all,' she replied with a laugh.

'Good.' He studied her face. 'Look,' he leaned towards her, 'tell me to butt out if you like but I get the feeling you're running from something or someone. I . . . I'd want you feel you can talk to me anytime you feel you want to unload on someone.'

'Do you?' She met his gaze, deliberated for a few seconds then said, 'Well, yes, I . . . I've left a marriage that was less than it should've been and I've come as far away as possible.' She studied the plastic placemat in front of

31

her before looking at Matt. 'It's not general knowledge . . .'

'Fair enough. It goes no further,' he said. 'My offer still stands though.'

'Thanks.' She looked at him and saw honesty in his eyes. 'I . . . I appreciate that.' She smiled then said, 'What about you?' She rubbed a fingertip on the tabletop. 'I've heard that you . . .'

'Libby Belling.' He shook his head, a wry smile tugged at his lips.

'Please, don't be cross with her, Matt. She, well she's . . .'

'I know. She's Libby. No,' he sighed. 'I'm not cross.'

'There's been no-one since?'

'There's no-one in my life, not any more. No-one that matters enough.'

'I'm sorry.' Amy brushed a finger against his hand. 'We both have some baggage then.'

'Some,' he agreed. He watched Amy as she sat opposite, pensively sipping from her cup. 'Is there anything else bothering you?' He stretched out one long finger and let it lie lightly against her wrist. There were shadows beneath her eyes and her manner was slightly abstract, more so, he thought, since her conversation with Sid Dacre. It was one of the reasons he'd decided to call at her house. The sagging floor he mentioned was genuine enough but little things were calling him to attention, concerning him about her welfare. It was a long time since he been so conscious of a woman in just this way. He tapped her wrist with his finger, reminding her of his question.

'Um, sort of,' she replied with some reluctance. She felt awkward. How could she tell him she thought she had seen a pair of . . . ghosts. Dreamed of them! For the first time she dared put a name to her feelings and she felt a tremor pass along her spine.

She glanced at him as she placed her cup back on its saucer. His eyes were serious, but the corners of his mouth were slightly tucked in as though ready to break into a smile. She was aware too of his touch where his finger rested against her skin. It felt good.

'Do you believe in ghosts?' The words tumbled from between her lips. She felt her cheeks burn, waiting for his reaction. Steeling herself against his laughter.

'Go on.' His expression didn't alter.

'Do you?' she insisted.

This time he grinned, forced into giving an answer. 'It's possible there's something we don't understand. Possibly an echo from the past that reverberates in certain conditions.'

'But not, "real live," ghosts, so to speak,' she said, sketching conversation marks in the air and pulling back slightly.

'Is that what's bothering you? You think you've seen a ghost?'

She liked him for not laughing at her. She decided to trust him. 'I'm pretty sure I've seen a couple. I saw them the first day I came to look at the house. They were rounding the corner of the house. I called out and then ran after them, but when I reached the back of the place no-one was there.' She looked at his face half expecting to see a derisive grin but there was none, just his eyes watching her steadily.

'Go on,' he told her. 'What else has happened?'

'I dream of them,' she said. 'It's that photograph I found of the same couple, on the floor half wedged beneath the skirting boards of the back room. Sid Dacre identified them and said their name was Tunney and they'd died years ago. There are voices too, in my dreams.' *Dear Lord, I must sound pathetic.* She kept doggedly on. 'They keep calling someone. I can't make out who it is but they're calling out some name.' She stopped. Heart pounding she waited for his reply. His judgement. It was, suddenly, terribly important that he take her seriously.

'What do you know about these people, the Tunneys?' Matt slouched back against his seat, watching her face, seeing the tension it held. He was certain she believed in what she was telling him. Convinced she had seen ghosts.

'Nothing really,' she said, feeling a little foolish. 'The estate agent just said they had owned the property and it's just been left pretty much as is after they died. There's a great-nephew, or something that lives in the

34

Northern Territory, that inherited it and leases it out, but no-one's lived there for some time.' She shrugged.

'Might be an idea to do a bit of research,' Matt suggested. 'Find the last tenants and find out why they left, etc.'

'What about the couple I saw though?' Amy leaned forward, her lightly clenched fists on the table.

'Probably a couple of old dears out for a stroll and got a fright when you turned up. Probably thought they'd get pinched for trespassing.' He turned the corners of his mouth downwards. 'People in small places like this tend to dress similarly, and what they have they stick to until it falls apart. It would explain why your ghosts looked like the Tunney's photograph.'

But not how they managed to disappear so quickly. She sighed, let her hands fall into her lap and her shoulders sagged. 'You could be right, but,' she raised dark eyes to him, 'I think I will make a few enquiries just the same.'

Amy gathered up her coat while Matt approached the desk to pay their bill. As she turned a shape passed the steam smudged window and for long seconds she froze. *Idiot*, she rebuked herself. For a fraction of time the shape had reminded her of Max, and she felt a surge of anger for her foolishness. How much longer was he going to be able to keep this hold of fear over her? *How much longer am I going to ALLOW him to do this to me, more like it? It's finished. Get on with life girl.* She drew a deep breath and squared her shoulders.

It was still raining when they pulled up in front of her house. She felt drained and was pleased when he decided against crawling beneath the house to inspect the floor and its supports. Too much mud, they'd agreed. There was no further mention of Amy's ghosts, but she knew he sensed her agitation and would willingly stay if she asked him to. Instead he merely ran a finger down the side of her face and along her jaw line.

'I'm fine, Matt.' She made herself smile at him.

'Call me if you need me.' He didn't smile in return, just watched her face.

'I will, I promise,' she said, wondering what he was thinking. She'd watched him go out the door and listened until she heard the sound of his car drive away. She made her way to her bedroom and lay on the bed pulling the heavy crocheted rug up over herself and listened to the rain on the tin roof until she dozed off to sleep for the next two hours.

CHAPTER FIVE

Amy patrolled her back yard the next morning, hands clasped around her coffee mug for warmth. She looked at the tiny green tips of bulbs pushing the heavy earth aside; struggling for space in the matted grass. A prelude of spring their bright display of daffodils and jonquils let run riot over the years had now spread with abandonment throughout the yard. Sipping at her coffee she welcomed the sun's pale warmth on her face.

A piece of straggling wire close to one of the willows caught her shoe halting her progress. She glanced down. *Good a spot as any right here.* She propped herself against the willow and watched the thin trickle of water make its way along the shallow runnel that had once been a creek bed. Drainage pipes installed some distance away had diverted the flow elsewhere, leaving a mere reminder of what used to be. A wave of irritability swept over her. She had come to Bingurra for a new start in her life. No Max, no reminders. Only to think she'd seen ghosts, then panic because a shadow reminded her of her ex. *Stop dithering. Start looking for information about the Tunneys and settle this thing once and for all.* Squaring her shoulders she moved away from the supporting tree trunk and turned back to the house, almost tripping in a shallow dent in the grass.

*   *   *

Amy's first visit was to the agent from whom

she'd leased the house.

'Sorry, love,' Tom Floyd droned at her, tilted back in his swivel chair the better to ease any strain on the paunch bulging over his trouser top. 'We had a bit of a fire here, oh must've been fifteen years or so ago. Lost a lot of our old records. Is there any special reason?'

'Not really, I just wondered.' Amy, disliking the way his eyes appraised her backed out the door before she could be asked any further questions. She made her way across the road to Tom's only competition, Alec Kander, where she again found herself none the wiser.

Alec Kander was eighty if he was a day, wiry and fitter than Tom Floyd at half his age. 'I never had business dealings with the Tunney's,' he told Amy. 'They gave their business to Floyds.' He sniffed indicating his opinion of their choice. 'And,' he called, as again Amy moved to leave, 'to the best of my recollection that place hasn't been lived in for close on twenty years. People don't seem to like it. Didn't Tom mention it?' His eyes snapped with what Amy could only call malicious laughter.

'Thanks anyway,' she mumbled and left.

*   *   *

Lessons over for the day, Amy visited the town's small Library and began her search, using one of the library's two computers and stored editions of Bingurra's newspapers not yet committed to film. Any snippets she found she noted down on a piece of paper for further consideration when she reached home.

Her evening meal finished, dishes washed and cleared away, Amy sat down to decipher her notes in orderly fashion, half regretting her refusal to join Matt, Libby and the red-haired football captain, in a night out at the currant "in" pub to listen to music supplied by a group of local youths.

With a forefinger, Amy pushed her reading glasses back along her nose. Drawing her note-pad closer, and with her pen at the ready, she began deciphering her scrawl from the creased piece of paper.

She sat back and glanced over her work, a rueful twist to her mouth. Her gleanings hadn't amounted to much. She had, after some delving, discovered that the last tenants of the house had been in the nineteen-seventies. They were named Fleming. Frank and Marie Fleming. An obituary notice in one of the old newspapers she'd flicked through had caught her attention. A Frank Fleming and his wife, aged in their fifties, had died when their car hit the side of a bridge and plunged into the river at the edge of town. They had no family, nor could their few friends shed any light on any travel plans they may have had. As the car was piled with luggage, it was assumed the

Flemings were going on holidays.

Amy grimaced, disappointed with her meagre findings. Still it puzzled her, why would the Flemings set out so late at night, even if they were going on holiday? She'd never heard of anyone deciding to leave in the middle of the night, plus how come none of their friends were acquainted with the fact of their going away? It struck her as most odd, and she made a note of it in the back of her notepad.

From old records she formed a scrappy picture of the Tunneys. William Tunney, aged twenty-four, had married Lucy Gardener, aged twenty-two, at Bingurra Registry Office in nineteen hundred and one. They had a daughter, Gladys, born to them in nineteen hundred and two.

She would have to wait until she could return to the Library and settle herself to go through old newspapers again before anything more could be added to her list. It was a time consuming exercise that made her eyes ache, but yet intrigued her.

A gust of wind rattled the windows making her jump and snapping her hard won concentration. Getting up from her chair Amy walked along the passage to the front end of the house and looked into the room. Cold white moonlight threw an outline of the French doors along the floor, casting the house bricks she had piled at their base in lieu of the chair, into shadow. She had hired a man due to arrive tomorrow and attach sturdy bolts to the tops and bottoms of both doors. 'Let's see any trucks shake you open then,' she sternly addressed the stolid, unresponsive frames.

*   *   *

'Georgie! Georgie!' The voice called shrill and wild.

Amy sat up in the dark, clutching at the blankets. A nameless dread filled her. She had dreamed again. The same figures and sense of urgency. The babble of voices, indistinct, as though spoken under water. Then suddenly, the piercingly clear call of the woman, 'Georgie!'

Cold air swept into the bedroom and across her head and shoulders. Fighting a sudden temptation to huddle in a bundle under the blankets at the foot of her bed like a frightened child, Amy placed one bare foot then the other over the side of the bed and on the mat. She fumbled with cold toes for her slippers, hardly daring to take her eyes from the doorway.

Holding the front of her pyjamas close to her chest in a tight grasp, she moved cautiously from her room and across the narrow passage to the open doorway opposite. The French doors, as she knew they would be, were again flung wide. The restraining bricks scattered

41

across the floor.

For a long moment she stood staring, shaking with cold and who knew what else, until her teeth began to chatter. *Truck vibrations? I think not.* The noise of her clicking teeth galvanised her into action and she crossed the room to shut the doors with a force that caused the glass to rattle.

*   *   *

'There yer are, lady, herd 'a elephants couldn't get that door open now,' the workman told Amy next morning as he stood back and surveyed the stout bolts now attached to the metal frame of the French doors. He was young, not more than twenty, but had all the promise of that rarity now-days, an excellent tradesman.

Covertly his curious eyes examined Amy. Not bad really. Considering her age of course. He'd opine she must be nudging thirty. He rather liked the way one curl of her hair escaped its clasp and corkscrewed down her forehead and bounced each time she moved her head.

'It's not elephants I'm worried about,' Amy mused oblivious to the appraisal she'd just been given. 'It's great. Just what I wanted.' She smiled at him, her hair haloed by the sun breaking through the clouds and slanting into the room.

The young man began to entertain thoughts of being invited to stay for a cup of coffee when the imperious call of the telephone interrupted. Within seconds it seemed, he found himself outside the house, tool-bag in hand and the door firmly shut against him.

CHAPTER SIX

'Come in, Libby,' Amy called out in answer to her friend's wave as she passed by the kitchen window.

'Oh yum!' Libby eyed the still hot tray of scones and sniffed the air, but her obvious and barely contained excitement had nothing to do with the prospect of eating freshly baked scones.

'Well?' Amy widened her eyes at her friend. 'What is it that's got you practically jumping out of your skin?'

'It's Jim. Jim Casey,' Libby added unnecessarily. Her green eyes deepened to emerald and a pink stain crept along her neck and stained her cheeks. 'I . . . uh . . . we . . . Do you like him, Amy?' She made a production of selecting a scone and dropped it on to her plate, avoiding Amy's gaze and waited for an answer.

'Seems a nice enough feller.' Amy narrowed her eyes at Libby, one hand close to her mouth hiding the grin she felt spreading across her face. 'Go on,' she ordered. 'What are you getting at?'

'We . . . Jim and I . . . have known each other for ages. I told you.' She flashed a look in Amy's direction. 'We've been out with friends, been to a few parties together at various times, but . . . uh . . . lately we've been seeing each other more often, as a couple you know. We get on really well together as friends and now it's a bit more than that, quite a bit.' She blushed, her fingers twining together. 'He . . . he's . . .' she stuttered, her sight fixed somewhere above Amy's head, 'asked me to go away for the weekend.' She lowered her eyes in time to watch Amy's eyebrows climb almost to her hairline and her cheeks reddened even more. 'It's to his family's place,' she defended, chin high. 'They live on a property just out of Llumley. Amy,' she lowered her voice to almost a whisper, 'I think he's going to propose!' She gulped in air and at the same time popped a piece of scone into her mouth and almost choked on the crumbs. 'I just had to talk to someone,' she said when she'd regained her equilibrium.

'And?' Amy fixed a teasing eye on her. 'Will you accept?' She'd not been blind to the obviously growing closeness between the pair and was pleased for them.

'Too right.' Libby was forthright in her answer and nodded her tousled blonde head vigorously.

'A toast!' Amy cried, raising her teacup, regretting she had nothing more appropriate for them to drink. They toasted Libby, and Jim who, she had finally discovered, as well as football captain, was actually an accountant and doing quite well, thank you very much. Their excitement raging high they added Amy's scones and anything else that sprang to mind to their list of toasts.

Hilarity eventually subsiding, Amy studied Libby for a quiet while then said, 'You've lived in Bingurra nearly all your life, Libby. Have you heard any rumours concerning this place?'

'What do you mean?' Libby pushed away the sudden unwanted thought that perhaps she was mistaken about Jim's intentions, and dropped the half eaten remains of her scone back on her plate. Her face took on a carefully neutral expression. 'There are always rumours of one sort or another in any place.'

'Don't beggar the question, Libby.' Amy's expression warned that she was no longer in the mood to play games. She watched Libby with steady eyes. 'I mean this place, this house.' Her voice was brisk as she pointed a finger floor-wards first then up towards the ceiling.

'I don't know.' Libby shrugged, suddenly awkward with her cup and saucer. 'I think there used to be some talk years ago, when I was a kid. But I haven't heard anything for

45

ages,' she said her voice defensive.

'What sort of talk?' Amy leaned forward. 'For goodness sake, Libby,' she said in clipped tones, 'you must realise I have a reason for asking, so don't try and play dumb with me.'

'All right.' Libby sighed and pushed her plate away and began speaking hurriedly, not liking the snap in Amy's speech and anxious to get it over and done with. 'The place was supposed to be haunted,' she said, and missed the soft sigh from her friend. 'I don't know what it was. I remember, when I was little,' she added thoughtfully, 'people talked about a car crash that killed someone that lived here, and that no-one could bear to stay here since.' Her bottom lip hovered between trembling and a pout. 'I didn't say anything to you because you seemed okay, and I saw no reason to frighten you, especially as you're on your own and it's pretty quiet down here.' She sat with lowered eyes for a while and when Amy failed to speak, lifted her head. Her face blanched and shock was in her eyes. 'You've seen something haven't you? Oh, Amy! What is it?'

CHAPTER SEVEN

Amy sank on to the sun-warmed grass at the base of one of the willows edging the once-was creek. She settled between the tree roots, allowing them to cradle her thighs in a makeshift seat.

She sipped from her mug of tea and tilted her head to gaze at the delicate green tracery descending along the long slender branches of the willow. The heavy sweet smell of wattle drifted across and mingled with the scent of blossoms. The faint hum of bees, industrious with their pollen gathering soothed her, letting her relax against the tree trunk and enjoy the soft warmth of the sun.

She let her mind drift back across the last two weeks. A smile creased her cheeks as she recalled Libby's return from her weekend with the Caseys, triumphantly flashing a diamond ring on her left hand.

Matt had arrived that weekend and donned a grimy pair of combination overalls before disappearing beneath the house, possible now the rain had eased and the ground dried out to an acceptable degree. 'Now is as good a time as any to check on the floor in the middle room,' he'd told her. 'If it rains again it could be weeks more before I can get under there.'

'Go to it,' Amy said and had waited, perched on a convenient stump, placidly listening to the thumps and banging noises coming from beneath the house accompanied by the occasional grunt and muffled curse when, she suspected, Matt's hammer had come into contact with flesh rather than wood.

He'd finally emerged covered in dirt and

cobwebs. 'At least two stumps need replacing, possibly more. I've been able to prop them up but it's only temporary,' he warned as he brushed a cobweb from his hair and spat dust from his mouth. 'You'd best see Tom Floyd next time you're in town.' He brushed a grimy hand into the front pocket of his overalls. 'Here, I found this as well.' He dangled a piece of black string from his fingers.

'What is it?' Amy wrinkled her nose as she took his find, wondering at the clump of mud attached to the string, surprised to feel it rested heavily on her palm. Curious, she rubbed her thumb across the messy lump and felt something firm in its centre. 'It feels as though there's something solid here,' she said, turning the article over and prodding at it with a finger. 'Hang on a minute.' She dashed inside and grabbing a small enamel dish, filled it with water and dropped her gift into it. 'Come on in,' she called through the window. 'I'll give it a scrub later and see what comes up. It's probably an old medal by the feel of it,' she said as Matt's tall frame filled the doorway. 'Here have a seat.' She pointed to a chair with a muddy finger. 'The kettle's on, I'll get us a drink and a piece of cake.'

'That looks good.' Matt eyed the chocolate cake as Amy placed a piece on a plate close to his elbow. 'There's a play on over at Willoughby if you'd like to go,' he spoke around his piece of cake and waggled enquiring eyebrows at her. 'It's a local production, but I hear it's pretty good, and tonight's the final.' He washed his cake down with a generous gulp of tea. 'If you'd care to, I thought we could have supper afterwards, to round it all off properly. Make a real night of it.' He helped himself to another cup of tea from the still warm pot and waited for her answer, hoping too for another piece of cake.

'Lovely.' Amy smiled her pleasure at him and placed more cake on his plate. Willoughby was a half-hour drive away and half the size again of Bingurra. It also boasted several places reputed for their cuisine. Besides, the idea of an evening with Matt wasn't unpleasant either, despite her firm resolve to keep their relationship on a friendly basis. She shuddered at the thought of being rejected because he was still grieving for his lost love. She was still far too fragile to sustain further hurt. 'But I should be the one taking you out for doing this.' She pointed towards the floor.

'Rubbish. This is reward enough.' Matt popped the final piece of cake into his mouth and ran his tongue around his lips ensuring no crumb escaped.

The evening had been every bit as enjoyable as Amy hoped. The play, a modern comedy had made them laugh, setting the mood for the rest of the evening. They'd had a light supper, their conversation centred mainly on the play and Amy took care not to mention anything

49

about the noises she heard at night. She was loath to discuss anything that would mar the pleasure of the outing and was grateful when Matt made no reference to it either. They reached her home and walked to her door in companionable silence.

'I'll say goodnight then.' Matt smiled down at her and she wondered if she'd heard a slight question in the word.

'Yes, goodnight, and thanks for a great evening, Matt.' She ignored the possibility of a question and returned his smile before producing her key and putting it in the lock.

Bending Matt dropped a light kiss somewhere between her cheek and the corner of her mouth. She thought she detected a minute hesitation, as though that hadn't been his first intention. 'See you,' he said as he turned away.

'Night,' was all Amy could manage past the thumping of her heart before she entered the house and found her way to her bed, suddenly feeling cheerful and relaxed. She woke the following morning to the realisation that she had experienced the most peaceful and undisturbed sleep she'd had in weeks.

*   *   *

'Hello Mr. Floyd,' Amy greeted the estate agent.

'Hello to you young lady.' Tom Floyd sat

50

a little straighter behind his desk. 'What brings you here? Problems with the house?' He looked closely at her, trying to read her expression.

I've a list of things here that need attention,' she told him. 'It mainly concerns the state of the foundations. They're practically all in need of replacement, especially those beneath the room with the French doors and the room directly behind it. That room in particular is in dire need of work.'

'Well now, let's have a look at that list of yours.' Floyd held out a pudgy hand and read, his lips moving silently. 'I see,' he said when he finally looked up at Amy. 'You've got yourself quite a list here I must say.' He frowned looking at the piece of paper in his hand once more. 'Well we'll see.' He folded the paper in half.

'You'll see? What does that mean?' indignation in her voice. 'Do you think I'm making it all up? I can assure you Mr. Floyd that I am not exaggerating in the least.' She folded her arms across her midriff and glared at him.

*   *   *

Within days it seemed Amy found her class workload was suddenly consuming more time than usual. Almost the whole class had handed in assignments apparently written in foreign

51

languages and completed with indecent haste. The reason, she knew full well. Firstly there was a sudden upsurge on the student social calendar with the appearance in town of 'The Lurid Lizards' one of the latest and most popular noise making, tonsil wrenching groups to have hit the pop charts this year. Then there was the fevered approach of the upcoming inter-schools football finals, an event the townships of Bingurra and Willoughby looked forward to down to the last man. So it was that the object Matt had found beneath the house and passed on to her, sat unattended in its dish of water for more than a week until the following Saturday when Amy finally got around to paying it further attention.

Tipping the muddy water out of the dish, Amy replaced it with fresh water and a little detergent. An old toothbrush in hand she began to scrub cautiously at the item. Bit by bit the well entrenched grime began to come away revealing a now blackened silver chain that broke in two places in her hand despite all her attempts to be gentle.

'Hello, what have we here?' Amy looked closely at the oval shape attached to the chain. It was not, she could see, a medal which had been her first thought, but a slender locket, with traces of entwined leaves still faintly visible on its pitted surface. 'Somebody's lost treasure it looks like.' She'd examined it closely but was unable to prise it open and afraid to press too hard in case she broke it. With great care she had run the point of a fine needle between the two edges then rubbed an oil soaked piece of cotton wool around it before placing it on a flat dish and leaving it to sit for a day or so longer wrapped in the greasy cotton wool.

This morning she had again, tentatively tried to lever the locket open, pleased when the two sides had, with grating protest, finally parted. With a soft dry cloth she slowly wiped the inside of the locket, surprised to find the picture it contained still recognisable despite its rotted and discoloured edges.

Standing where the light was best, she examined the photograph. She saw a young woman, her hair parted on one side and extending across her head in rigid waves. A Marcel Wave, Amy believed it was called, vaguely recalling having seen them advertised in old magazines kept by her grandmother. A hairstyle popular in the nineteen-twenties and thirties, she thought. The woman's face wore a closed look, with thick dark eyebrows adding certain heaviness to the features. The mouth was surprisingly full lipped but unsmiling, its corners pinched tight.

Amy felt a wave of sadness sweep across her as she examined the picture. She turned the locket in her hand to see the back of it but there was no clue as to the owner, and she placed it on the ledge above the sink before

53

making herself a cup of tea and carrying it outside to enjoy the spring sunshine.

Eyes closed she let her body respond to the languor of the day, until feeling chill she opened them prepared to move now the sun had gone. But the sky was still blue and the light coming through the willow's budding green leaves, bright. Puzzled she lowered her gaze and looked towards the house. Her breath left her body with a whoosh. She felt weak and all but paralysed. Close to the slight dip in the grassy yard where she had almost tripped, stood the woman in the dark hat and coat. Her eyes were fixed on Amy in an angry stare.

Desperately dragging air into her lungs, Amy tried to find her voice but produced only a rough croaking noise. Then the woman was gone. The air warm and redolent once more and the humming of the bees sounded again in her ears.

CHAPTER EIGHT

With a spasm of irritability, Matt pressed the remote control and silenced his television set. Frowning he regarded his sock covered feet resting at the far end of the couch. He felt uncomfortable, verging on guilty, as if he'd been prying. Well, so he had in a way. No, he corrected himself, not prying, listening to gossip, not intentionally but nevertheless he had listened and heard something he felt uncomfortable about. Next time, he promised himself, he would heed his instincts.

It was ten years since his class had graduated. Bits of paper clasped in curled fingers to show the world they were now qualified to teach its children, confident they could send them out into the world prepared to cope with all the stress and strains they would inevitably encounter.

'Let's have a reunion, in, say, ten years. See what marvels we've wrought in that time.' Someone, he couldn't remember who, had suggested and cheerfully they'd all agreed. Matt had forgotten about it until his invitation arrived a week ago.

'Go.' His married sister had commanded him from Melbourne, when next they'd spoken over the telephone. 'Stay here with us and have a catch up with Richard and your nephew and niece as well.'

'I've lost touch,' he said. His first impulse had been to refuse the invitation.

'Rubbish,' was the brisk reply. 'You can't hide yourself away in the country forever Matty. You've got to get out and mix with people again. People you've known for years and maybe even a few new ones.'

'I'm not hiding,' he said with indignation. 'I'm perfectly happy here and I have a good social life and new friends.'

'Matthew.' He heard the warning in her voice and meekly submitted.

'Alright! Alright! Anything if it'll stop you nagging at me.' He heard her chuckle. 'And it will be good to catch up with Richard and the kids.'

'Atta boy. We'll look forward to seeing you. Bye sweetie.' He heard the click as the call was disconnected and half sighed and half laughed. Paula had always been the bossy one. Older than Matt by three years she'd taken over as leader during their childhood and never relinquished her grip.

He'd gone to the hotel in Melbourne, where a room had been booked for the occasion. He stood on the perimeter of the crowd watching the backslapping and pseudo-modest, and sometimes blatant, claims that grew with each round of drinks.

'Matt? Matt Armstrong?' Matt turned to look in the direction of the speaker.

'Peter Grant,' he said with the first really genuine smile of the evening. The two men shook hands grinning in a slightly embarrassed manner at each other. During their final year Matt and Peter had become good friends, and for some years afterwards had exchanged cards at Christmas, ceasing as each moved and addresses became lost.

'Brisbane?' Matt's interest was pricked. 'I know someone who taught just out of

Brisbane, in Yeronga. Do you know it?'

'I taught there for two years,' Peter laughed. 'Who is it you know?'

'Amy McKenzie,' Matt said. 'Though McKenzie is her maiden name, she reverted to it after she split with her husband.'

'Amy.' Peter nodded his face suddenly void of amusement. 'She tell you anything about her old man?'

'No.' Matt shook his head. 'She just said she'd been married and they'd broken up. Bad was it?' he probed, disquieted at the expression on Peter's face.

'Bad's not the word for that bloke.' Peter shook his head. 'He's a real nutter. A control freak. More than once I saw Amy with bruises on her arms, it doesn't take much imagination to think of other places she must've been bruised at times. Even after she left him he wouldn't leave her alone. She took off in the end without telling anyone where she was going. If Max ever gets wind of where she is I don't like her chances.'

'He'd still follow her?'

'Too right. I told you, he's a nutter. Completely obsessed with her.'

*   *   *

Amy drove to Matt's house, still trembling a little over the appearance and worse, the disappearance, of the woman in her yard. Matt

57

answered her rapid tattoo on his door and invited her in, and if he looked a little less than his usual self she failed to notice. Unsure of how to begin her tale, she had enquired firstly about his weekend away.

He'd not answered her immediately, taking his time before he turned from the kitchen bench, a mug of coffee in each hand. 'Here,' he said, placing one of the mugs on the table for her and easing himself into the nearest chair. 'I met a good friend of mine at the reunion. Hadn't seen him for years. You know how it is.' He saw her nod in reply. 'His name is Peter Grant.' And he watched as her face flushed with colour then drained, leaving her pale and looking ill.

'I suppose my name came up,' she said, feeling hollow inside.

'I'm sorry, Amy,' he said. 'It was just one of those coincidences. Peter said he was in Brisbane and it followed on from there. I didn't mean to pry into your life. And I thought twice about saying anything to you, but I figured you'd find out one way or another, and I'd rather be the one to tell you.' He wished her face didn't look so washed out under the tumble of dark hair. 'I didn't mean to pry into your life, Amy. I thought we were good enough friends by now that you could trust me.'

'Of course,' she answered. 'It'd be odd if my name hadn't come up I suppose. Don't worry about it. As you said, it was just one of those things.' She bit her bottom lip, feeling tears threaten and was angry with herself for giving way.

'Amy it's true then?' Matt's voice was gentle. 'About your husband knocking you around?'

'I thought . . .' her voice wobbled, 'I thought not mentioning the violence, no-one else would think about it, and it would be easier for me to forget.'

'Oh God. Amy,' his voice pained, he put out a hand to her, hurt as she withdrew without actually moving.

'It's all right, Matt. Really. It's just . . .' she put her half finished mug of coffee on the table, 'I think I'll leave, we'll both feel a bit uncomfortable if I stay.' She turned to the door, pausing before opening it. 'I'll see you at school.' And she left, not telling him of her reason for calling in the first place and climbed into her car while Matt watched, swearing softly to himself for the whole mess of it.

Amy stormed into her kitchen, tossed her shoulder bag at the kitchen table, not bothering to acknowledge the clunk as it skidded across the table and landed on the floor, but instead headed for her bedroom where she flung herself across the bed's broad expanse.

Matt hadn't laughed at her story of seeing ghosts, even if he was less than convinced, but now . . . Amy had seen it before. People who knew of Max's treatment of her. The stalking and her reaction to the dead cat left on her doorstep. They put the slightest sign of stress down as hysteria, if not downright paranoia.

'And who could blame the girl after what she's been through?' Amy had overheard a couple of her aunt's friends discussing her one day when they thought her safely out of the room. Her aunt had defended her vigorously, bless her, but Amy knew people were not convinced. And now Matt knew! How could she talk to him of ghosts?

Angrily she gritted her teeth. *I'll do this on my own. I'm perfectly capable. I have the odd brain here and there . . . I hope. I'll find out just what has happened here. Something dire must be the cause of these noises. These happenings. This haunting! There is no other word to describe it. After everything I've suffered at Max's hands I can surely deal with an angry old lady and a few voices. Nothing,* she clenched her fists tightly in the rumpled bed sheets, *neither Matt Armstrong nor any ghost is going to scare me off.*

'Do you hear that?' she yelled at the room. She closed her mind to the near breathless panic she'd experienced when she had seen the woman standing in the yard glaring at her. *What is she so angry about? Does she resent anyone living in what has once been her home? Is she connected to the voices?* Amy mulled the thoughts over, feelings of relief washing

60

over her with the realisation that since the new bolts had been fitted the French doors had remained closed through the night. She occasionally heard whispering sounds but sternly told herself it was the soughing of the wind through the trees. *Yeah, right!*

The voice calling for Georgie had been absent lately, and she hoped it had stopped for good. But there was no denying this house had a ghost, and she was determined now to get to the bottom of it.

*   *   *

Three weeks after Matt's reunion in Melbourne a group of friends gathered in a Brisbane pub to celebrate the forthcoming nuptials of one of their mates. And celebrate they did, leaving the prospective bridegroom perched naked on a toilet seat in one of the cubicles, his wrist handcuffed to the cistern pipe, grateful only for the warm weather that prevented him from dying of the cold as well as embarrassment.

Peter Grant was one of the roisters and discovered to his great and inebriated joy that he knew the man standing next to him at the bar. 'I've met you before.' His bonhomie was expansive. 'I was jus' discussing a mutual friend of ours a while back with a mate I hadn't seen for a long time.' And as the man he addressed paid for the bottle of wine

61

he'd purchased, Peter grabbed at his sleeve, leaned closer and said, 'Amy McKenzie,' in triumphant voice.

The man stiffened and fixed Peter with a hard look. 'What do you know about Amy McKenzie? How do you know me?'

Peter grinned happily. 'Met you when Amy taught at the same school as me. Think she lived with you and your wife for a while.' He suppressed a gentle hiccough. 'Went to a reunion down in Melbourne and met a mate who's teaching at the same school as her now, in the country.' He wrinkled his brow and widened his eyes in anticipation of his companion's pleased surprise, to find himself suddenly alone as the man brushed roughly by and left the hotel.

The part-time barman whose ears pricked at the mention of Amy's name, made a mental note to be passed on later to another source whose interest was undoubted.

*   *   *

Having decided on marriage, Libby saw few reasons for delay, and had plunged into wedding plans, her enthusiasm sucking others helplessly in like a huge vacuum cleaner. It was the reason she and Amy were now ensconced at a rear table at the Bill 'n' Coo, bridal magazines scattered around their meal.

'Can you think of where else I might be

able to get information about the Tunneys?' Amy, tired of looking at fatuously simpering brides and their attendants posed in incredible attitudes on the glossy pages, asked her friend.

'Um . . . you could try the Historical Society,' Libby replied, sparing Amy a glance while keeping a finger firmly placed on the picture she'd been examining.

'What Historical Society?'

'There's one over at Willoughby.' Libby nodded over her sandwich, anxious to get back to her magazines.

'I doubt my house would be on their agenda,' Amy said dryly, but looked thoughtfully at the preoccupied face opposite her. 'And if it isn't, there's not much hope they'd know anything about the Tunneys.'

'Maybe,' Libby said with a shrug. 'But even if they're not interested in doing anything about the house itself, it is old and they are bound to have looked at it at one time. There's always someone that knows what went on when,' she grinned wickedly, 'and it's a wonder Madge Thornton, at the Library didn't mention it.'

'Ah, well,' Amy sighed, 'I did only ask what was available here in Bingurra. Silly me.' She laughed, and knowing this part of the conversation would go no further, pulled the nearest magazine towards her and returned to the discussion of wedding gowns and all the accoutrements.

In Brisbane Max Harrelson nodded briefly to the man behind the bar.

'Hey Max, got a minute?' the part-time barman called.

'Yeah, what is it?' Harrelson looked at the man over his shoulder.

'I've got something I think you'd be interested in.'

'Like what?' Harrelson turned towards the barman.

'We had a buck's party here last night.'

'So?' Harrelson scowled. 'What's that got to do with me?"

'Well they were all pretty well plastered as you might guess but I heard one of them talking to a bloke used to be a friend of your missus.' He saw Harrelson's already surly countenance become dark and his heavy eyebrows draw together across the bridge of his nose.

'What about her?' His voice took on a threatening tone and the barman wished he'd not mentioned the subject.

'He knows where she's living.'

'What?' Harrelson took a step closer to the barman, one fist gripped the man's shirtfront. 'What did you say?" He shook his informant and nearby patrons discreetly moved out of the way of any danger.

'Easy Max,' the barman tried but failed to free himself of Max's grip. 'I heard him tell this bloke that he'd met someone at a reunion and that Amy's living in Victoria.'

'Is that so? What town?'

'Dunno Max, honest,' he quavered. 'All I know is it's somewhere in central Victoria.

'What makes you think I'd be interested in where she is anyway?' Harreslon let go the man's shirt and took a step backwards, hearing the thudding of his heart and kept his eyes downcast lest his informant note the bright light in them.

'Dunno,' he repeated. 'I just thought I'd mention it, like. I gotta go, Max. See ya.' The barman pushed his way through the door behind the bar and hurried out of the building where he busied himself for a time shifting crates from one spot to another, leaving the second barman to cope with the clientele and wondering if he'd done the right thing.

CHAPTER NINE

'Tunney?' The voice said over the telephone. 'I really can't say off-hand, but actually, you may just be in luck, dear, some of our members are in Bingurra today. They're inspecting the old school, if that's of any help to you.'

'Thanks,' Amy replied. 'I know where that

is. Do you have any idea of what time they're to be there?'

'Sorry, I can't help you with that, but I should think around eleven-ish might be a good time,' the voice tried to be helpful.

Disappointment and frustration mingled in Amy's breast as she trudged away from the old school and the three members of the Willoughby and District Historical Society.

'Which house?' 'Who?' 'Where?' they'd said, one after the other.

'Don't recall ever having heard of people by that name,' said the narrow gentleman with the tucked in chin.

'We've never been to that part of Bingurra. I'm quite positive of that,' said the buxom lady in the ruffled blouse, adding that she was Secretary of the Society, which Amy supposed put the seal on it all.

'I'm new,' said the third member, peeping at Amy between the shoulders of the others.

'Well, thanks for your time anyway.' Amy dredged up a smile before turning away to begin her walk back home, considering the only pleasant aspect of her day so far, was the warm sun and gentle breeze.

She turned the corner stepping from the rough gravel of the side road on to the smooth footpath of the Bingurra's street, glad of its feel beneath her shoes. Further along she could see Alec Kander, sitting on a bench outside his business, his legs stretched out to the warmth of the sun.

'Morning.' Amy nodded politely as she came level with him and received a nod in reply.

'Just a minute, Missey,' his voice came after her, and she slowed her step and half turned to face him.

'Yes?' She stood still, waiting. *Missey*?

'You're the one came asking about the Tunney's old place, aren't you?'

'That's right,' she said knowing he was perfectly aware of who she was.

'Did you have any luck?'

Her mind racing, Amy took a step sideways, bringing her fractionally closer to him. Given Alec Kander's age, he just might be able to give her some information. But would he? He was well known for his cantankerous turns of mind, so why bother to ask? But then, he was obviously curious about something, why else would he bother to speak to her?

She took another step and placed herself next to him. 'I found a few bits and pieces, nothing much, really.' She watched his eyes. 'I found where a couple who used to live there were killed when their car ran off the bridge one night.' She paused but he just sat looking under his wrinkled eyelids at her. 'I thought it curious that they chose late at night to go on holiday,' she said slowly, still watching him.

He nodded but said nothing.

She tried again, 'All I could find out about

67

the Tunney's was the date of their marriage, and the birth of a daughter.'

'Have you looked in the cemetery?' His smile made her feel half-witted.

'No,' she said. 'Is it worth it? Headstones don't usually say much except, Born, Died, and Beloved of, etc.'

'You might find it interesting.' Again he gave the grin she found so irksome.

She waited, but apparently that was all she was going to hear today. She had the feeling that Alec enjoyed stringing things out as far as possible. She stepped away from the old man and said, 'Thanks, Mr. Kander, I'll have a look at the cemetery.' She omitted to add she had little faith in discovering anything other than that already stated. She walked off, her opinion of people, mainly Alec Kander and the three she'd left at the old school, rating none too highly. She thought of Matt Armstrong and sighed. *Dratted man.*

After her initial upset over Matt's disclosure, Amy had calmed down enough to admit she'd known from the first minute he'd spoken he had nothing to be blamed for. He had simply been embarrassed about hearing of her marital problems from somebody other than herself, and thought it better to be up front about his knowledge. Her own hot reaction, well, she shrugged, it was all a mixture of pique, embarrassment, and irrational fear that, somehow, somebody in

Bingurra knowing would be to her detriment. 'Idiot,' she told herself under her breath. 'Matt's not an idle gossip, and would never hurt you deliberately.' Still the thought sat uncomfortably in her mind.

She and Libby were at their usual table for lunch the next and last, day of term. Looking between the people clustered about the other tables, Amy could pick out Matt, leaving the queue at the food counter, and cowardly she began examining the contents of her sandwich.

'Matt.' Libby called his name, and forced to lift her head, Amy saw him approaching their table in response to Libby's signal. 'Where are you off to?' Libby asked, pushing a chair towards him.

'I've got a lot to sort out before the end of the day.' Matt ignored the chair and stood at the end of the table, sandwich and drink in hand.

'Not that much surely? Come on, sit down and eat your lunch with us.' She gave the chair another shove.

'Thanks, but I really do have to go.' He backed off with a general wave in their direction and disappeared through the canteen door.

'Well.' Libby stared at the disappearing figure then swivelled suspicious eyes at Amy. 'Had a wee spat, have we?'

Amy felt herself colour. She had intended to make her peace with Matt, but not in

69

front of Libby, and Matt hadn't given her the slightest opportunity of gaining his attention before taking off like a rocket. 'Not really,' she said, trying to appear off-hand. 'Just a bit of a disagreement.' Her fingers fiddled with her coffee cup. 'He probably is busy anyway,' she said more firmly, trying just as much to convince herself as Libby. 'I know I am and so are you.' She looked at her friend who wisely, hunched her shoulders and let the subject drop.

Amy had gone looking for Matt after classes ended for the day, wanting to apologise for her behaviour and explain to him, but his class room was empty and a passing teacher, seeing her standing in the doorway, told her he'd seen Matt leaving almost immediately after the bell had sounded. 'Gone away for a few days fishing, I think.'

So here she was, on her way to collect her car and visit the cemetery, probably on a wild goose chase, and wanting to right things with a man who'd deliberately gone fishing to just annoy her, she was sure, and also very aware that she missed his company. She'd been surprised at the realisation of just how much more she appreciated his companionship these days. 'Now that he's not here, of course,' she muttered to herself, striding towards home and her car.

Bingurra cemetery lay on the outskirts of town, almost a ten-minute drive. Its blue stone and iron surrounds were liberally sprinkled with lichen, and one gate leaned back against the fence, its upper hinge snapped through the matching gate missing altogether.

Amy stood in the entrance and looked around wondering where to begin looking. It wasn't a large cemetery compared to those in the cities. *Got rather a cosy feel to it actually. If you can call such a place cosy.* Some of the graves with their neat surrounds looked rather like well-made beds. A double row of large pine trees lined the main pathway, their tops leaning inwards to touch against each other. She could smell fresh cut grass and saw a vacant ride-on mower against the far fence, its occupier gone for lunch, she presumed.

Where to begin? The graves seemed to be a haphazard jumble of old and new. She decided to divide her search into sections and progress row by row.

She had been at her quest for almost an hour, peering at headstones, stepping across unmarked graves, unable to stop feeling heartache at some of the inscriptions, especially those for children. 'I'll just go home none the wiser and depressed into the bargain,' she scolded herself softly, and then she found it.

Close to a side fence, almost covered by a tangle of wild grass and weeds and sheltered by an old pine tree the grave laid untended, it seemed, except for the occasional council tidy-

71

up. The headstone sat grey and crooked at one end of the grave, its face pitted and weather-beaten.

Carefully Amy knelt next to the low mound of earth. She picked up a sturdy looking twig fallen from the pine tree and gently scraped at the moss-stained headstone.

WILLIAM JOHN TUNNEY
1897–1967
LOVED HUSBAND
of
LUCY GARDNER TUNNEY
FATHER
of
GLADYS
ALSO
LUCY GARDNER TUNNEY
1899–1969
LOVED WIFE
of
WILLIAM
MOTHER
of
GLADYS

Amy let her breath out on a long sigh as she stood up and brushed the dirt from the knees of her jeans. The inscription on the headstone was what she had expected to find. Names and dates of when the Tunneys had been born and died, nothing more. 'I haven't yet heard of anyone having their tombstones inscribed with whether or not they're going to come back and haunt their homes and why,' she addressed the head stone. 'Is that what you're up to?'

Cross with Alec Kander for sending her on a fruitless trip, she was about to turn away when a small lizard, disturbed by her presence, scuttled past causing her to jump, the heel of her shoe hitting the headstone and dislodging something from behind.

Bending sideways to see, Amy found a small oval piece of granite lying in the dirt. It must have stood directly behind the larger stone and become dislodged when her shoe hit it. She turned it over and stood frowning down at the inscription. It was quite easily read. Its face, turned into the headstone had been protected from the ravages of time and the weather.

IN LOVING MEMORY
of
GEORGE ARTHUR TUNNEY
LOST AUGUST 1936
AGED 4 YEARS

Her pulse racing Amy stared at the plaque. *Is this what Alec Kander sent me out to find? What does it mean? Lost. A rather odd way of recording a death or did George Arthur Tunney, aged four years actually become lost?* She read the inscription again. *Poor little mite.* Her mind pictured his fears and cries. The frantic search

73

by his parents. Parents?

She brought her imaginings under control and did some rapid ticking off on her fingers. Little George would have been born in 1932. That would make William and Lucy well into their fifties, too old to be the parents, and there was no mention of George on their headstone. Gladys then. George must belong to Gladys.

Amy rubbed her chin with a dusty forefinger, leaving a pale smudge behind. George. With a start she realised the voice that disturbed her at night cried out for 'Georgie.' Her heart skipped a beat. Were the Tunneys still looking for little lost Georgie?

Where was Gladys? Amy did some mental arithmetic. Gladys would be in her nineties, now and it was possible she was still alive, but if so why would Alec send her all the way out here and if Gladys was dead why not come out and say so? Why hadn't he mentioned the little boy?

Guess who's coming to call, Alec Kander. She gritted her teeth as she turned back towards the cemetery entrance and wishing more than ever that Matt Armstrong was close by.

'Well? Find it then, did you?' Alec looked up as Amy's shadow fell across him where he still sat on the bench in front of his business.

'Yes.' Amy sat down beside him. 'You could've just told me instead of all this rigmarole,' she said, a tinge of exasperation in

74

her voice.

'Could've.' He nodded agreement and smiled, leaning back against the wall.

'What about Gladys?' Amy asked. 'Is she still alive?'

'Nope.' Alec watched dust motes swirl about the toes of his shoes.

'Well what happened? When did she die?" Amy clenched her fists inside her pockets, controlling the urge to reach out and wrap her fingers about the old man's scraggy neck.

'Oh a long time ago.' Alec appeared to be calculating, but Amy knew he was just prolonging things. 'I guess,' he said at length just before she reached screaming point, 'Gladys died in . . . oh . . . I'd say nineteen-thirty-three-ish.'

'Oh.' Amy sat quietly by his side absorbing this information. 'So William and Lucy, the grandparents, took Georgie did they?' She felt sadness descend on her.

'Didn't take him. Was given him.' Alec chuckled a vile phlegmy sound.

'What do you mean "given him"?' Amy bit her bottom lip in vexation. 'What happened Mr. Kander?' She really was going to choke him in a minute.

'Ah, well.' He'd had his bit of fun and enjoyed it, now he'd tell what he knew. 'You've been hearing strange things, haven't you?' He watched her face.

'Yes.' Her skin prickled. 'The French doors

open. I hear voices. I've . . . I've even seen them.' If he laughed again she would burst into tears.

'Have you just?' He turned a surprised gaze on her. At last she'd impressed him. 'Well, well. There's been people come and go in that place. The voices drive them out.' This girl had staying power, and he raised her a full notch in his estimation. 'Tom Floyd tries to keep it hushed, but word gets about. People just don't stay more'n a few weeks. Those two killed in the car crash,' he looked to see if she followed, and continued on at her nod, 'they stuck it out for nearly three months. Must've been something pretty awful to scare 'em enough to take off in the middle of the night.'

Bet they saw William and Lucy. Amy kept her mouth firmly closed, waiting to hear what else he had to tell her.

'I was only a lad at the time,' Kander continued, 'but I remember the Tunneys. Always dressed in black. Had their own ideas about religion. Used to spend all day Sunday in prayer, I think. They were pretty strict with Gladys. I remember her well. She was quite a few years older'n me,' he shook his head, remembering, 'used to pass me on her bike, going to work at Pratkin's Drapery Store when I was walking to school.' He jerked his thumb in the direction of the old school the Historical Society had visited earlier in the day.

'I remember the gossip when she got herself

76

hooked up with one of the lads at the store.' He gave a phlegmy chuckle. 'The young feller had a reputation as a bit of a Jack the Lad, and he got poor Gladys pregnant. I believe there was a hell of a to-do when her parents found out. Mind you,' he said with a twist of his mouth, 'Gladys was about thirty then, and I reckon she must've thought it'd be her last chance at getting married.' He snorted a laugh. 'Anyway, the bloke shot through and her folks threw her out.' He held up a hand to halt the words about to tumble from Amy's lips. 'Dunno where she went, but she turned up on their doorstep again months later with this new baby. Even then they shut her out. Hard they were, so Gladys parked the kid on their front verandah and went and chucked herself under a train.'

He turned and looked at Amy, sitting with her hands tightly clasped in her lap her face pale. 'Some people can do things like that and still call themselves Christians.' There was no hint of laughter in the old man now.

What happened then?' Amy had trouble finding her voice. 'Is Gladys buried in the cemetery? I didn't see her grave.'

'Dunno,' Alec answered shortly. 'In those days a suicide couldn't be buried in consecrated ground, and I didn't bother to find out. Too young to know much then, or care. I found out most of it as I grew older. Anyway, the Tunneys kept the little feller,

77

and then one day he just disappeared. Nearly sent them mad. People searched for miles, even probed an old miner's hole in their back yard in case he'd somehow managed to fall in, but they found nothing.' He sank back on his seat, suddenly seeming to have lost his spirit. 'Are you satisfied now, Missy?' He glanced up beneath baggy eyelids. 'I suppose you'll be moving out now, like the others and looking for somewhere else to live.' He gave another phlegmy cough.

Amy got to her feet, realising she and the old man were now sitting completely in the shade, and it was getting late. 'Thank you, Mr. Kander,' she said quietly. 'You've been a great help. And no,' she shot him a look from under her brows, 'I'm not intending to move out.' And leaving him still seated on the bench, she climbed into her car and set off for home.

CHAPTER TEN

Max Harrelson ran his finger along the roads marked on the map, concentration etched on his features as he traced the route he would follow. One finger marked his present position in Brisbane, another followed along the marked highway, clear through New South Wales and down into Victoria. If his information was correct Amy was living in a small country town in the State's centre. It could take some time, but if he were precise he would be successful. Amy was a trained secondary teacher so deleting towns without high schools would save him considerable time.

He had thrown in his job a week ago and spent the time making preparations for the journey. He would drive the long distance. It would make it easier to bring Amy back, than trying to get her to board an aeroplane if she decided to be recalcitrant. She really would have to learn that she simply couldn't run off like that, he thought. She was his and had to stay with him.

He'd totally disregarded the divorce, he considered it inconsequential. He became angry and upset when the police had tried to interfere in what he deemed to be his personal business. He'd watched her with relentless attention, waiting until she came to her senses and returned to him, suitably repentant of course, and fully understanding the necessity of him having to punish her. Then she had disappeared. Completely. But now he had a good start in the right direction, and he would find her. Of that he had no doubt.

Smiling he folded the map and placed it in his pocket. Bending he picked up his sleeping bag, closed and locked the door of his house and walked to his car. He threw the sleeping bag into the car's boot and shut the lid.

Getting into the vehicle he started the engine and humming to himself, he pulled away from the verge and onto the road. He was happy. He was going to bring Amy home.

*   *   *

It was freezing in her bedroom. Amy's exploring fingers came away moist when she brushed them across the quilt. She could hear the voices beginning again. A soft, indistinct murmur barely noticeable at first, but gradually becoming louder and clearer. She could hear the urgency in the cries. Then the rattling noises began in the other room, gently at first then increasing into a frantic shaking.

Heart thudding, her nerves on edge, Amy screwed up her courage, threw back the blankets and crossed the narrow passage to the opposite room and switched on the light. It was cold in here too, and the French doors shuddered and strained against the newly placed bolts holding them closed.

'Stop it! Stop it!' She leant against the frame of the door, her hands covering the sides of her face, tears starting from her eyes. 'Just cut it out. I'm not frightened of you and I'm not leaving,' she shouted her defiance. 'I'm sorry about Georgie, and I'm sorry about Gladys, but it's not my fault.' Exhausted she leaned against the door to the room her hands limp by her sides.

For the space of a few seconds the silence was absolute, then a sharp noise made her jump. Across a glass pane in one of the French doors there appeared a long diagonal crack. Amy waited, but nothing more happened. The room was still cold but no longer felt threatening. It seemed to be waiting. Waiting for what?

Nervously she moistened her lips. 'I went to the cemetery today. I found the grave and Georgie's plaque.' She paused and felt the room was listening. 'I've got the locket too. The one with Gladys' picture in it. Matt . . . my friend found it under the house.' The silence felt heavy and she hurried on. 'I don't know what happened to Georgie, either, but I'm sorry for you.' She debated whether it would be wise to mention Gladys' name again and decided against it. Better not to push her luck too far. Instead she stayed quiet and was aware of the temperature in the room slowly beginning to rise, and a feeling of acceptance seeped into her.

Perhaps now they know I understand their grief and will allow me to get some sleep at night. She made a moue at the thought.

Shivering she made her way back to her bed, cold now where she had flung the blankets aside. She snuggled under the quilt, trying to get back to sleep and marvelling at her outburst and its surprising result.

81

*   *   *

'Heard from Matt?' Libby asked Amy the following morning, slanting a glance at her friend seated beside her.

'No,' Amy tried to sound nonchalant, not looking at Libby but keeping her eyes fixed on the road ahead.

'You didn't patch up your fight, did you?'

'It wasn't a fight.' Amy squirmed at the accusation. 'Just a bit of confusion, really. He'd already left the school and was gone from his house by the time I got there,' she said, sounding indignant in her effort to justify the omission. 'How much longer before we get there?'

'Half an hour, and don't try to change the subject.' Libby was not about to be distracted with trivial questions. She tightened her grip on the steering wheel of her little red car as it bounced along the unmade road towards the nearest large town. They were intent on scouring as many shops as possible for further items she considered essential to her forthcoming nuptials, this time in the manner of lingerie.

'I'm not changing the subject.' Amy eased her position in the front seat. 'There just isn't anything more to say. Matt was gone by the time I reached his place. I haven't heard from him and I don't know where he is.' She was beginning to feel irritated with Libby's

82

attitude. *Such a carry-on.*

Sensing her friend's discomfort, Libby acceded graciously. 'Okay, consider the topic closed. Tell me instead how you got on with the Historical Society.'

'Ugh. They had nothing to tell me.' Amy screwed up her nose. 'So I went to see Alec Kander and from there, at his suggestion, I went on out to the cemetery.'

Libby listened to Amy's tale, sighing over Alec's story of Gladys and her baby, and caught her breath as Amy told her of the peculiar happenings in her front room that night.

'How can you bear to stay there? No-one else has been able to stand the place. How come you're sticking it out?'

'I don't know.' Amy gnawed at her bottom lip. 'It frightened me, it truly did, and for a while I thought I really was going mad.' She gave a jerky laugh. 'Realising that I actually had seen the Tunneys was almost a relief. Perhaps they want someone to help find Georgie, or what happened to him. My telling them that I know what they're on about seemed to settle things down a bit, but what more I can do, I don't know.'

'I don't know either,' Libby said, swinging the car past a roundabout as they entered the town and headed along the main thoroughfare. 'But back up a bit. Why would you think you were "really" going mad?' She'd caught the

83

unconscious emphasis Amy had placed on the word.

Realising her gaffe, Amy sighed and swallowed hard. 'I suppose I'd best tell you. Matt knows. It's the reason for our upset,' she shook her head, 'and I guess it's only fair to tell you. Find a café somewhere first, I need coffee for this.'

Libby heard Amy out, saying nothing, but her emotions registered clearly on her face. She broke her silence only when Amy's voice dwindled away. 'You've divorced him, Amy,' she reached for her friend's hand, 'he can't pretend even to have the slightest claim on you, and he'd have no idea of where to look for you anyway.'

'That's what upset me so much when Matt told me about his friend.' Amy looked miserably at her companion. 'This Peter Grant, he teaches in Brisbane. He doesn't know Max, I know, but with him in the same town it's all just a bit too close for comfort.' She shivered as though a chill breeze had swept across her. 'All this is partly why I've stayed at the house. I'm simply tired of running, and after last night, I don't think I'm frightened of the Tunneys anymore either.' She rubbed her temples with her fingertips, trying to discourage the headache that threatened to spoil her day.

'But how?' Libby asked leaning forward. 'All Matt did was mention to his mate that he

84

knows you. Your ex has no idea about any of this, and I'd say it's highly unlikely he'd ever find out. How could he?'

'Murphy's Law.' Amy gave a short laugh. 'Max would need only the slightest inkling about anything and he'd be onto it like a bloodhound.'

'Come on,' Libby pushed her chair back and stood up. 'What we need is some solid Retail therapy . . . for both of us.' She linked her arm through Amy's and together they exited the café and turned their attention to the original purpose of their day's outing.

Amy and Libby completed their shopping and oddly enough Amy found she'd enjoyed the occasion more than she'd thought likely. They had dissolved into fits of giggles over the more risque articles of lingerie on display in some of the shops with Libby finally settling for delicate but more conventional items. And Amy wondered if part of her relaxed enjoyment was due to her unburdening herself to Libby. Whatever the reason, they had made the most of their day and not returned to Bingurra until almost dark. Amy let herself inside the house, too tired to bother with anything more than a hot shower, before seeking her bed. No amount of noise from the Tunneys could keep her awake, she told herself, and hoped with all her heart it would not be put to the test.

CHAPTER ELEVEN

Matt eyed the petrol gauge on the dash of his dark green Ford, happy to see it registered a remaining good half tank. No need to worry about finding a service station for a while yet, although his windscreen was becoming cluttered with squashed insects and dust. He felt relaxed and refreshed after his week by the river. His brother-in-law Richard had telephoned unexpectedly, his annual fishing trip was due and one member of the party unable to come.

'I know the school holidays are starting and thought you might like to fill in the extra spot,' he'd said and laughed when Matt jumped at the opportunity.

Hasty preparations had given Matt little time to ponder over Amy, and he'd been obliged to depart the instant his classes ended.

Two hours driving took him to the New South Wales border with another good two hours yet to be completed. Richard had promised to meet him at the turn-off to the camp and guide him through the last few miles of darkened terrain.

His features creased in happy recall as he ably manoeuvred his motor over the bumpy road. Tents and camp beds had been set up on the riverbank and he'd settle in comfortably with the other anglers. Everyone, he was informed, took it in turns to cook. A day's fishing completed with yarns and a few beers about the camp fire at night before turning in. Nothing, but nothing, smelled or tasted as good as bacon and eggs cooked over a camp fire in the open air, unless it was the aroma of their own freshly caught fish, and all of it washed down with mugs of Billy tea. It was the best holiday he could remember in years.

When Matt was twenty-three he had become engaged to be married. He'd known Carmel since they were kids practically. Had been sweet on her forever. He was twenty when they began going together on a steady basis and he smiled now at the gentle memory of her.

It had been at her birthday party that they'd announced their engagement and planned to marry a year later. When Carmel was killed in a collision between her car and a petrol tanker, Matt thought his world had come to an end. All he wished for was that he had been with her, for what was life without his love? It was a long time before he believed he could once more have a normal life.

He had taken other women out since, of course, formed real friendships with some, but that had been all, until now. Amy, he was aware, was creeping into the spot he thought he had sealed off forever. They'd formed a warm liking for each other, he'd enjoyed their time spent together, and the evening they had seen the play at Willoughby had felt so comfortably right. But it wasn't until he saw her reaction to his news about meeting with Peter Grant and their conversation, that he'd wondered why he felt the way he did. His anger at the idea of someone treating and abusing her so, and a pulling at his gut at the obvious fear he knew she hid beneath the anger at his revelations. She'd avoided him for days and to his regret he'd made no obvious effort to seek out her company.

Uncomfortable at the direction his thoughts were taking Matt was pleased to have to concentrate more on his driving as the car ahead of him slowed and pulled to the side of the road when they approached the border with its signs warning of penalties incurred by the taking of fruit across the line.

This is obviously a conscientious bloke and no doubt an upstanding citizen, As one is! Matt chuckled as he passed the stationary vehicle and crossed the border back into Victoria. He was totally unaware that it was not conscience that brought Max Harrelson to a halt, but the need to avoid all possible risk of drawing unwanted attention to himself, especially by something as trivial as carrying illicit fruit into another State. Neither did he know that when Max Harrelson discovered who Matt was he'd be next after Amy on Max's list.

Max Harrelson now trailed the dusty green

Ford along the bitumen highway, losing it only when they approached an intersection and the green car turned right. Max looked at the signpost and after a moment's deliberation took the left turn on to the road towards the town where he planned to begin his search for Amy.

He had examined his map carefully, selecting towns with a High School. He would begin in the centre of the State and work his way outwards in widening circles. With his pen he had numbered the towns in order. He had marked Sunfield first, wavering between Stockton to the left of it and Willoughby to the right. Decision made, he marked Willoughby second then placed a black number three beside the name of Bingurra.

*   *   *

Amy looked at her watch, surprised to find it was past lunchtime. She had spent over four hours at the Library, peering at old copies of the 'Bingurra Express' for articles concerning the death of Gladys Tunney and the disappearance of Georgie.

Fat lot of good that was. Stifling a yawn she stood up from her chair and switched off the machine she'd been using and gathered up copies of the paper not yet digitised, ready for return to the front desk. She folded the copies she had made into her bag and left the

Library. She needed coffee and lunch, and in that order, before she did anything more about the mysterious disappearance of little George Arthur Tunney, over sixty years ago.

CHAPTER TWELVE

'Max Harrelson has disappeared.' Sarah Stanford looked at her husband her dark eyes wide.

Greg paused in the action of placing his briefcase on the hall table before loosening his tie and stared at his wife. 'How do you know?'

'Iris Pilbruk told me,' she said, twisting her fingers around each other.

'Who?' Greg scowled trying to place the name as he walked into the bright living room of his home, divesting himself of the constricting trappings he wore for his day at work.

'Iris Pilbruk,' Sarah repeated the name for him. 'We go to the same hairdresser. She was there today and mentioned it.'

'Slow down, slow down.' Greg waved a calming hand at his wife. 'How does this Iris person come to connect you . . . us . . . with Max Harrelson? And why would she feel we should know he's disappeared?' He fixed his wife with a stern gaze and saw her cheeks redden.

90

'I know her from meeting her at the hairdresser. We seem to have our appointments at pretty much the same times.' She bit her underlip. 'We often talk, and I found out she lives near Max Harrelson. She read about him in the paper, about his stalking Amy, and the cat thing.' Sarah's eyes flashed at the memory.

'You discussed Amy's business with a stranger?' Greg felt anger at Sarah's indiscretion begin to seep through him.

'No!' Her reply was immediate and indignant. 'You know I wouldn't do that, Greg. Iris hasn't even mentioned him since then and neither have I. It was pure coincidence that we were both having our hair done today, and she . . . Iris . . . said that she had seen Max load his car up and take off a week or so ago and he hadn't come back yet. She notices, more I think, because of his past record. Sort of keeps an eye on him I suppose.'

'Well, I'm sure there's no need to panic.' Greg's irritation subsided and he attempted to soothe his wife's worries. 'If there's no 'For Sale,' sign on the house he's probably just gone on holiday. Even people like Max Harrelson take a holiday now and then.'

Sarah searched his face for reassurance and was almost satisfied. 'Could we telephone Amy anyway? Just to be safe?'

'Better not, we just might be scaring her for no good reason. She doesn't need that.'

91

Greg hugged Sarah to him. 'There's no way he could find her, you know that, love. As far as Max Harrelson is concerned, Amy could be anywhere, even overseas.'

'Yes. I suppose I hit the panic button,' she said, a little shamefaced. 'But that man really gives me the creeps, Greg.'

Greg Stanforth patted his wife's shoulder before moving into the bedroom in search of a pair of shorts. He was not as complacent as he had tried to sound. He knew where Max Harrelson worked and would see what he could find out—whether Max had gone on holidays, and if so where, and if not, what?

*　　　*　　　*

Amy sat at her kitchen table and scanned the spread out photocopies she had brought home from the Library. There was one brief report on Gladys, all she had found despite a thorough search. It consisted of one small paragraph near the bottom of a page, stating that the body of a woman had been recovered from the train tracks half a mile out of Bingurra, and it had been identified as that of Gladys Tunney, aged thirty-three. Amy scanned following editions of the newspaper carefully without finding any further mention of Gladys Tunney.

She stared at the brief clipping for a long moment, her mind picturing the misery and despair that had driven the woman to such a desperate act. Poor thing. Poor Gladys. And she wondered how the Tunneys, William and Lucy, had felt when told the gruesome manner of their daughter's death. *Was that why they kept the child instead of placing him in an orphanage? To atone for their feelings of guilt at having rejected Gladys, not just once, but twice? Their ceaseless searching and plaintive cries for Georgie. Did it mean they felt they'd failed yet again, or had they come to love the little boy and their grief doubled at his disappearance?*

The sun sent a splash of warm gold through the kitchen skylight to sprawl across the papers and Amy's hands resting on them. She placed the article about Gladys to one side and shuffled through the remainder.

CHILD MISSING

The headlines were thick and dark. It had been big news, and the search had lasted for days. A blurred picture of the Tunneys, snapped during the search for Georgie showed Lucy, one hand held in front of her face in an effort to ward off the invasive camera. William, his shirt unbuttoned at the neck, a long thick stick in his hand looked gaunt and exhausted.

Lucy had discovered Georgie missing from his bed when she had gone to wake him from his afternoon nap. A search of the house failed

93

to find him and Lucy called William from where he was working in his shed. The one with the padlock on it, next to the garage, Amy guessed.

It was William who realised Georgie must have escaped through the French doors, pushed together but no longer latched. Lucy had been working in the kitchen, the child could not have got past her unseen, and the large key locking the front door and still turned to the locked position was far too stiff and heavy for small fingers to manipulate. But the catch on the French doors was light and well oiled due to their frequent use, and a footstool close by showed how the little boy had managed to reach high enough to manoeuvre it open.

'Used to fancy himself being able to walk out on to his front verandah without having to use the front door.' She recalled Sid Dacre telling her about William Tunney the day he'd inspected the French doors.

Amy sat back imagining the frantic search, the hopes and fears of those looking for little Georgie Tunney. She read on. The countryside was scoured, far and wide but no trace of little George Arthur Tunney was ever discovered. Again, Amy heard Alec Kander's voice. 'They even probed an old miner's hole in the back yard in case somehow he'd fallen in.'

Miner's hole, Amy mused. It wasn't unusual to find disused mine shafts in people's back yards, front yards either, for that matter. The whole area was well and truly dug up in the days of the gold rush. Most of the old shafts were later filled in and their locations either lost or forgotten about, coming to light only after torrential rains caused them to cave in, sometimes a hundred years later.

Amy shivered with the realisation that the slight dip in the yard she managed to trip over almost every time she crossed to where the willows grew must be the shaft referred to. She would, she promised herself, take good care from now on to avoid that spot, even though she was aware it would have been filled and capped with concrete.

'Amy.' The voice made her jump and she squinted against the bright sunlight at the dark figure outlined in her doorway.

'Sorry if I startled you,' Matt said as he stepped just inside the room, so she could see him more clearly.

'Matt,' she heard the pleasure in her voice as she left the table and moved towards him. 'You're back.' She gave herself a swift mental kick. *Of course he was back.* 'I'm so pleased.' She couldn't believe it. She was gushing. Still she burbled on. 'I wanted to see you, to apologise for that day. It was unfair of me. I couldn't find you after school and you had left by the time I reached your place.' The spurt eased and she felt hot colour suffusing her face and neck. He had caught her off-guard.

It was always one of two things when that happened. Either she rabbited on or clammed up completely. *Idiot.*

He stood still, his hands hanging loosely by his side his eyes clear and fixed intently on her face. A tiny smile tugged at the corners of his mouth. He didn't seem to mind her verbosity in the least.

Looking at him, Amy found she was suddenly breathless, she felt weak and unable to move, aware only of a tingling over her body and a small pulse that beat rapidly at the base of her throat like a butterfly trying to escape its confines. A slow heat began spreading upwards through her body and she felt as though her knees were about to give way on her.

'Got the kettle on?' The prosaic words broke the spell, and only Matt would ever know the effort it had cost him, with her standing there, hair haloed by the sun from the skylight, and her eyes wide upon him. Her lips were slightly parted and he could see the throbbing in her throat where a pulse flickered emphasising the creamy softness of her neck. What instinct held him back from crushing her against his chest, he didn't know.

'Um, yes, yes, of course.' She snapped out of her trance and took swift steps across to the stove to push the gently singing kettle further over the heat, glad of the opportunity to regain her senses.

Slowly, feeling as though she had experienced a sharp storm, Amy relaxed and sat facing Matt, watching him as he drank the tea she'd poured, listening to his account of the fishing trip, smiling at the recalled enjoyment that made his face crease with laughter, unconscious that beneath it all, Matt was finding it increasingly difficult not to slam his mug down on the table and pull Amy into his arms. Instead he flicked long fingers at the papers still strewn across the table, noticing the photograph of William and Lucy Tunney.

'Still searching?'

'Yes,' she said, sitting erect then leaning forward to tell him of the blank she'd drawn with the Historical Society, her conversation with Alec Kander and subsequent trip to the cemetery. She recounted Alec's tale of Gladys and her baby and of her family's refusal to help and her resulting suicide and the Tunneys rearing of Georgie until his disappearance.

'That's a can of worms,' Matt said with a grimace, then rifled through the papers before him. 'But I don't see what more you can do about it.'

'Well, for one thing, the Tunneys might stop looking for him and for another I'd like to know for myself what happened to that little boy. It seems so sad.' Concern registered on her face and in her eyes.

'For heaven's sake, Amy.' Matt raised his hands, palms upwards. 'Anything could have happened. He could have wandered miles away, it would've been pretty much all bush around here back then. He could've just been lost and lay down and died of hunger and exhaustion. He could have fallen down another mine shaft out there somewhere, or,' he concluded, not liking the distress that filled her eyes, 'he could've been kidnapped and is now somebody's fat old grandfather, sitting on a porch somewhere, without a clue that anything out of the ordinary had ever happened in his life.'

'No. He's dead.' She shook her head. 'And do you know, somehow I think the locket you found has something to do with it.' She felt as startled to hear herself say the words, as Matt appeared to be at hearing them.

After Matt's departure Amy returned inside and going to the centre drawer in the kitchen dresser, she pulled it open and looked down at the silver locket lying there, snug against her clean tea towels. Thoughtfully she picked it up and opened the case to look once again at Gladys Tunney's picture. 'I suppose all she ever wanted was to love and be loved, really,' she said under her breath, the sight of the long dead face evoked a heavy sadness in her.

She sighed and snapped the locket shut, bouncing it gently in her cupped hand while her brow furrowed in thought. How long had the trinket lain undiscovered beneath the house, and how had it come to be there in the first place? She'd had no inkling of what she had said to Matt concerning the locket, but on hearing her own words was convinced she was right. Somehow that locket was linked to the disappearance of little Georgie Tunney. *I wonder if the little monkey pinched it and took it under the house to play with?* She pondered. *Did he hear his grandmother calling for him, became frightened and left the locket there and then forgotten it? Or did he drop it and run off in a panic to avoid punishment and became lost?*

Screwing up her face in frustration Amy let the locket fall from her fingers back into the drawer and pushed it shut. She had other things to think about right now. She and Matt, with Libby and Jim were going to dinner and the pictures in Willoughby.

Feeling light-hearted with thoughts of the evening ahead she made her way to the bathroom and a hot shower, softly singing snatches of a song beneath her breath as she went. Her world was beginning to look pretty good these days.

*   *   *

'Thanks very much.' Greg Stanforth hung up the telephone and rubbed the palm of his hand against his jeans clad knee while he wondered what his next move should be.

Since his discussion with Sarah, he had gone out of his way several times to drive past Max

Harrelson's house. Each time he'd found it with blind covered windows, giving nothing away. It held an air of desertion which became more and more apparent as the small square of front lawn showed signs of neglect with its unkempt grass and rapidly sprouting weeds.

Greg eventually telephoned the place where he knew Max had been employed for the past year in the vain hope the empty house signified nothing more than a holiday or change of address. He would disconnect the call instantly if Max was at work.

'Max Harrelson?' the voice on the other end of the line asked. 'Um . . . just let me check, I won't be a moment.' Greg heard the clatter as the telephone was put down on something hard, probably a desk. His hopes were dashed when the voice returned minutes later saying, 'I'm sorry, you're out of luck, Max Harrelson resigned two weeks ago to go travelling. He left no forwarding address so I'm afraid I can't be of any help.'

'I see. Thanks anyway.' Greg replaced the receiver and chewed on his lower lip trying to think. He had admonished Sarah for jumping to conclusions and now found he'd been guilty of the same error.

He squared his shoulders. Max Harrelson had absolutely no idea of where Amy was, and no way of finding out, despite his threats to the contrary. Still it would only cause Amy unnecessary worry to let her know Max had disappeared.

He went outside into the brilliant Queensland sunshine and walked around the corner of the small house to the garden where Sarah was busy re-potting plants, and admired the rear view of her neat figure. 'Hey lovely creature,' he hailed his wife, 'how about we make up a picnic lunch and take it to the beach and spend a lazy afternoon?"

'What have you done or what is it you want?' Sarah sat back on her heels her dirt encrusted hands held away from her body and regarded her husband with suspicion.

'Nothing,' Greg assumed his most innocent expression. 'Can't a man take his wife for an afternoon at the beach?' He saw her look of scepticism and grinned. 'I just thought a drive to the beach and a picnic lunch would be good for us. You've been a bit uptight over this Max Harrelson thing and it might help you to relax a bit.'

'You're on.' Sarah laughed and got to her feet making shooing motions at Greg as she passed him and headed for the bathroom to tidy up before inspecting the contents of the refrigerator.

Greg smiled as he watched her depart and bent to clear away some of the pots still waiting to be attended while far back in the recesses of his subconscious was the dim reminder of the drunk who had spoken to him in a pub one night, weeks ago.

*   *   *

The same evening while Amy showered and readied herself for the outing, Max Harrelson locked the door of his motel room behind him and crossed the narrow space to where his car was parked. He would drive the short distance to Willoughby, see a movie, then find somewhere he could have a meal.

His search at Sunfeld had yielded nothing of any value. He had telephoned the two schools there, asking for Amy McKenzie, fairly certain she would have reverted to her maiden name, which was another black mark against her in his book, and received negative responses. He had spent the next four days, two at each school, unobtrusively stationed where he could clearly view the gates in case Amy should be there but under a different name, but there had been no sign of her.

And then there was the woman. He had picked her up in the pub one night and bought her a few drinks, accepted her invitation to return to her home where they had consumed most of a bottle of whisky. When the argument started he had beaten her, coldly, methodically, and viciously, and left her lying bruised and bleeding across the bed.

He'd thought it best to move on then, and made his way the fifty dusty kilometres further along the highway to Willoughby. Tomorrow he would renew his search.

Max wandered to the town picture theatre and sat through the film, only moderately interested in it. His thoughts constantly reverted to his errant wife and the punishment she would receive for the trouble she had caused him, both financially and emotionally. There was simply no way all this bother could just be ignored.

He left the theatre, hunger pangs momentarily dominating his mind. Fish and chips would be the order. Something he could take away and eat in the car, best not to be seen about too much if it could be helped. He threaded his way through the crowd, not bothering to look about him, and missed the foursome queued mere feet away, waiting their turn to see the film he had just watched.

CHAPTER THIRTEEN

The noise disturbed Amy's sleep. Slowly she drifted awake to realise she could still hear the sobbing that had been part of her dream.

Unmoving she listened, absorbing the fact that the room felt quite cold again. The noise was coming from the room opposite. Sighing she climbed out of bed, felt for her slippers and dressing gown and fumbled her way out of the bedroom.

Wearily she stood in the centre of the front room. It had been weeks since the last disturbance. Not since the night she'd responded to the voices, and the glass in the French doors had cracked. She was mildly surprised to find she no longer felt the terror that at first had overwhelmed her, but she was still far from feeling totally composed. Uncomfortable was how she felt. Very uncomfortable, and perhaps just a tad nervous to be honest.

The sobbing had scaled down to a softer note. Now they were deep wrenching sobs that seemed to come from in front of the French doors, close to the bottom, as if somebody crouched there while they wept.

'I'm sorry,' Amy whispered. 'I really am so very sorry.' She walked slowly back to her bed and pulled the covers over herself and lay there, listening until the weeping faded away.

*   *   *

It had been a wonderful evening. Libby had come in the car with Amy and Matt. Jim, already being in Willoughby for business reasons, was waiting for them at the restaurant.

'Jim,' Libby had greeted her loved one flinging her arms about his neck.

'How's my girl?' Jim had responded and hugged her close to him, while Amy and Matt smiled at the enthusiastic greetings as though the couple had been apart for weeks instead of a day and a half.

In the restaurant they'd eaten their meal and shared a bottle of good red wine, Amy listening good-humouredly as Matt recounted once again the highlights of his fishing trip. The conversation had then turned to Amy and her efforts to gain information concerning the Tunneys and the disappearance of Georgie.

'Give it up as a lost cause,' Jim advised. 'There's nothing more to be done, Amy.'

'No,' Amy cried indignantly. 'I can't give up yet. You ought to hear them. It's pitiful the way they keep calling out for him.'

'Guilty conscience, probably,' was Jim's caustic rejoinder. 'They chuck the daughter out for playing around, or getting caught more likely, and she killed herself, and then they lose the kid.' He pulled the corners of his mouth down and raised his shoulders in a shrug. 'Why don't you just move out? It must give you the willies, putting up with that racket night after night.'

'Do you think I'm making it up?' Amy's eyes sparked at him.

'No. No. Not at all,' he said quickly. 'You identified the Tunneys in that old photograph you found. You hear noises from the room where the little bloke got out of the house. I believe you, Amy, I just don't know why you stay there.' His eyes held genuine puzzlement

105

as they met her look.

'It's partly your fault I'm still there.' She grimaced at him. 'Yours and Libby's. You both knew the place was haunted but never said a word.'

'We'd heard rumours, but that was all.' Libby was quick to spring to the defence of her beloved. 'And you never said anything about ghosts or anything else out of the ordinary.' She regarded Amy with a wounded expression.

'I know. I'm sorry. It's all right.' Amy grinned and lightly patted her friend's arm before moving their conversation on to other matters, including the great football match to be played between Willoughby and Bingurra the following Saturday at the Willoughby football ground.

Amy and Matt had the car to themselves on the homeward trip. Libby snuggled herself into the front passenger seat of Jim's car and waved as they passed Matt and Amy soon after both vehicles moved off.

Matt killed the car engine when they reached Amy's front gate and walked with her to her door, waiting while she found her key and turned it in the lock.

'Well,' she looked up at his dark outline as she spoke, 'it was a great evening, Matt.' She couldn't read his expression in the shadows but she had the impression that his breathing was a little uneven.

'Amy.' He put his arms comfortably around

her. 'Are you frightened of being on your own here?' His soft breathing moved tendrils of her hair above her forehead.

'No, I'm not afraid.' Her heart began to hammer and the warmth of him was inviting. 'A bit nervous sometimes,' she said with a small laugh, forced to admit the truth, 'but not afraid, not any more. They're not out to hurt anyone, they just want to find Georgie.'

'I could stay if you liked.' His voice sounded rusty.

'Oh.' She felt the blood pound in her temples and her body began to tremble and she was suddenly very short of breath. 'I, oh . . .' She lifted her face to his and his kiss was firm and inviting, increasing in its intensity as it went on until she drew back, shaken with the force of her response.

'I'd like to stay, anyway,' he whispered close by her ear, his breath sending small shivers down her neck.

'No. No, Matt.' She fought for composure before looking up at him. 'Please, it's not you. You know that. It's just . . . not yet. I'm . . .' She floundered for words her mind scurrying for cover while her deceitful body practically jumped up and down on the spot shouting, 'Yes please!'

'It's all right.' Matt stood back a little from her. 'I guess it takes some time and I don't want to rush you. I'm willing to wait, if that's what you want.'

'Oh, Matt. Oh, yes, oh thank you.' *There I go again. Babbling away like an idiot.* Her only consolation was the dark of night concealing her pathos. But he didn't seem to mind, not judging by the way her kissed her again, he didn't anyway.

Shakily she smiled at him in the gloom and went inside before her willpower gave way and she flung herself at him, only to be humiliated when she froze at the crucial moment, as she knew she most probably would. It had already happened to her once, before she left Queensland, and she was not about to risk it again. Not until she was absolutely certain of herself. *Blast you Max, you did a good job on me didn't you?* She winced at the thought.

Amy had gone to bed, still warm from Matt's kisses and the feel of his arms about her, and slept peacefully until the sobbing had awakened her. Now she lay in the dim room recalling the night and waiting for sleep to claim her once more.

CHAPTER FOURTEEN

The late spring promise that warmer days were not far off had taken a backward step. The day was cold, icy rain stung any exposed flesh and ran down hard surfaces in driving rivulets, and soaked with relish into woolly hats and coats. It also saturated the Willoughby football ground and lay deceptively just below the grassy level, waiting for play to begin, for grass and soil to churn into a black sticky morass that would glue itself impartially to players of both sides.

Huddled into the collar of her coat, scarf hitched up to chin level and hat pulled well down to cover both brow and ears, Amy surveyed the area with dismay. Football was not one of her favourite sports, but the thought of not attending this game of games had never for one moment entered her head. The honour of Bingurra High was at stake.

She had travelled to the match in her own little car, bringing Libby with her. Jim, as well as captaining the Bingurra football team, was coach for the High School, and as such had been obliged to accompany the team to Willoughby in the bus provided for their transport. Matt, seconded far too easily as Goal Umpire, Amy thought, had also found it necessary to share the bus trip with Jim and the lads, not to mention the trainers, runners, and anyone else who could find a possible excuse to be included.

'Over here.' Libby tugged at Amy's sleeve, pulling her behind herself as she skilfully manoeuvred her way through the cluster of damp coats and dripping umbrellas towards one end of a row of seats encircling the oval and covered at intervals by a narrow roof. With an agility born of long practice, she aimed for a meagre bit of bench space, using her picnic basket as a wedge to secure a small space for herself that turned, miraculously, into ample room for two, and was reasonably sheltered from the worst of the wind driven rain.

Boldly Libby winked at Amy's expression of embarrassment. 'Them as can, do. Them as can't, get wet,' she said, grinning cheekily about her.

Grateful for the shelter, Amy gazed stoically ahead, comforted by the thought of the thermos of hot coffee inside the basket, and feeling sympathetic towards the combatants and their judges who were about to take the field.

*　　　*　　　*

Max Harrelson had also come to the Willoughby football ground. He stood with his back against the side of the refreshment kiosk, sheltering beneath its meagre overhang not far from where Amy and Libby sat. He sipped from a take-away cup of hot coffee while his eyes, peering from beneath the peak of his cap, scanned the clusters of people as they passed by.

He'd arrived in Willoughby too late yesterday to make enquiries about Amy, but signs outside the Willoughby High School advertising the forthcoming football match

110

had caught his attention, and despite knowing her lack of interest in the game, he had come on the off-chance that some quirk of fate had seen fit to place her there, within his reach. He deliberately stationed himself by the kiosk, and later on he would mingle with the spectators and look for her in the throng. If she was here, he would find her.

*   *   *

'Can we go now?' Amy nudged Libby's arm. The final siren had sounded and a jubilant Willoughby High had beaten Bingurra High by a mere two points.

'May as well,' Libby sighed. 'There's not much point in hanging around. The fellers will be in the dressing rooms for ages yet, and anyway they'll be going back by bus. We certainly won't see them before this evening.' She stood up, and again using the picnic basket as a wedge, began working her way back to Amy's car. A docile Amy squeezed past the large man in a bulky raincoat who'd stood behind her for almost the whole of the game, shielding her from view, and followed in Libby's wake.

Back in Amy's car the two women somehow managed to divest themselves of their wet hats and coats, tossing them on to the rear seat, grateful for the warm air that began circulating the enclosed space when Amy started the

111

engine and switched on the little car's heater.

Amy began manoeuvring to take her place in the slow moving line of vehicles heading in the direction of the gates, oblivious of the man waiting just outside the gates, watching the cars as they left.

Max saw the small green car make its way towards the gate, trying to get a clear view of the occupants as the windscreen wipers swung to and fro to clear the tumbling rain from the glass. Two local lads, celebrating their team's victory and tossing a football to each other as they ran through the rain cannoned into him. Off balance, Max stumbled, one foot splashing in a muddy puddle. He cursed the boy's clumsiness and by the time he'd regained his footing Amy's car was past.

The last of the cars gone, Max turned angrily away from the gate, feeling his foot squelch cold and uncomfortable inside his shoe. It was beginning to look as though he may have a long search on his hands, but that was all right. He could be patient if it meant finding Amy, and he was sure he would and was just as sure she would realise she had only herself to blame if he were to be irritable by the time he discovered her whereabouts. He would try the Willoughby school on Monday before moving on to Bingurra.

*   *   *

The dance in the Birragurra school hall began as a subdued affair, despite Sid Dacre's well intentioned speech commiserating with the school's football team and the school over their loss, but praising their gallant effort and asserting his faith in them for the final outcome the following year. Gradually youthful spirits rose and the hall filled with the noise of laughter and stamping feet as they gyrated to the beat of the band. Amy knew she would have a headache the next day.

Less than halfway though the evening, Matt declared he'd had enough of the cacophony. He could, he said, feel his throat beginning to tickle and his eyes were bright with the prelude to running a temperature. His stoic endurance at the goal posts seemed likely now to see him victim to a nasty cold.

*   *   *

'Sarah.' Greg Stanforth called to his wife from where he paced up and down his lounge room, passing the sliding door open to his patio, oblivious to the perfume carried inside by the warm evening air and the splendour of the bougainvillea outlined in the dim light.

Dutifully, Sarah popped her head around the door to stare at her pacing spouse. 'What is it Greg?' she asked, moving a little more into his view and revealing the long knife she held in one hand. 'I'm trying to make a salad out

113

here, what do you want?' She waved the knife with a mischievous smile.

'I met a drunk in a pub, a few weeks back,' he spoke impatiently, ignoring his wife's expression of pretended shocked surprise. 'He said he knew me. Knew Amy. They had taught at the same school.'

'Here?' Sarah's face was suddenly serious. 'And?' she urged her husband to continue.

'I can't think of his name. He said he'd met us, or me, anyway. Knew Amy had stayed with us.'

'I don't know. Nothing springs to mind.' Sarah scowled, trying to remember. 'Why is it so important?'

Greg ceased his pacing and turned to face her. 'Because he said he'd recently met someone else who knows Amy, and where she's now living.'

Sarah's face turned white and she leaned against the doorjamb for support. 'And Max Harrelson has disappeared, been gone for weeks.' She turned anxious dark eyes to her husband's strained countenance.

*   *   *

'Exactly.' Greg's voice sounded thick in his throat. 'I have to find this man, see who else he could have spoken to.'

'And telephone Amy,' Sarah cut in. 'Greg, we have to let her know.'

114

'Not yet.' He held out a restraining hand. 'Firstly I have to find this feller and sort out what's real and what was drunken rambling. Think, Sarah, think of the names Amy used to work with.'

Together they sat at the table, paper before them, Sarah substituting a pen for the knife they began cudgelling their brains for names.

CHAPTER FIFTEEN

Tom Floyd smiled expansively at Amy from his position by her back door. 'Been trying to get in touch with you,' he said, managing to convey that his appearance showed just how much trouble he was prepared to put himself to in order to please his clientele.

'Yes?' Perplexed, Amy waited for further enlightenment.

'I've got someone lined up to fix those wonky stumps under the house.' He inclined his head. 'Been on to the owner and he said to go ahead, so I'll have a man here first thing tomorrow.' His smile reeked self-satisfaction.

'Oh, thanks.' Amy looked suitably grateful for the information, though curious as to why he should come all this way to tell her in person.

'The telephones are out of order,' Floyd sated her curiosity. 'Went out last night, I hear.' He shifted his stance, his glance across her shoulder into the house clearly stating his wish to be asked inside.

'The 'phones are out?' She'd caught his look but was not about to invite him inside, instead she stepped outside, shutting the wire door behind her.

'Been an accident further along the highway. Bad one by the sound of it, and the 'phone lines have been brought down. A couple of trucks they said, anyway the 'phone lines have been brought down all over the area.' He eyed her, assessing, his feet braced slightly apart, his paunch straining against the rather dingy white of his shirt. 'Looks like it'll be some time before they'll be fixed. Most of the repair crews are over at Rippleby, trying to restore things over there after the big storm the other night.'

Amy nodded in understanding. The rain that made Saturday's football match so uncomfortable had been the edge of a severe storm that had left a wide and ruinous trail of damage in its wake, and Rippleby's telephone system was one of the worst casualties.

'Thanks for letting me know, Mr. Floyd,' Amy said with a nod and began walking towards the corner of the house, forcing Tom Floyd to follow.

'Tom. Call me Tom, my dear,' Floyd urged her with an ingratiating smile. 'This the spot?' He peered at the side of the house as they drew level with it.

'Yes.' Amy pointed to an area where the chimney jutted from the wall.

'Old Tunney's work.' The agent aimed the toe of one shoe at the brickwork.

'The fireplace?' Amy showed surprise.

'Yep. Rather fancied himself as a builder, from what I heard.' Tom smirked at her. 'Hooked up those French doors and then decided to put a fireplace in that room there. What for, I don't know,' he said, answering a question she may or may not have been about to ask. 'Ever use it?' he enquired.

'No.' Amy stared at the uneven chimney. 'I haven't bothered with it at all. Probably just as well,' she laughed. 'It'd more than likely smoke the place out. Anyway,' she swivelled on the balls of her feet until she faced him, 'thanks again for letting me know about the repairs.'

'My pleasure.' His eyes scanned her from head to toe in a quick flick that angered her, before he walked along the short, paved front path and through the picket gateway.

*   *   *

Still in Willoughby, Max Harrelson was also victim to the non-functioning telephone system and unable to make his usual calls to the school, had to content himself with watching the school gates both morning and afternoon. He would, he decided, stay in Willoughby an

117

extra day to be certain he hadn't missed Amy either entering or leaving the area.

* * *

'Peter! That's it.' Sarah Stanforth clutched at her husband's arm. 'I remember Amy introducing us to a Peter someone or other one day at the school. Oh, what was his other name?' She chewed her lower lip in vexation. 'Peter . . . ? No, no,' she muttered to herself irritably. 'Peter . . . that's it. Peter Grant.' Triumphant, she laughed at Greg. 'Quickly, get the 'phone book and look him up.'

'Oh, clever girl.' Greg said admiringly and gave her hair a friendly tug in appreciation as he passed behind her to collect the telephone book. 'Here it is.' Less than two minutes later his finger pointed to the name they sought, and Sarah copied the number on to a piece of paper, then followed him to the telephone and stood by his side watching while he dialled and waited for someone to answer.

* * *

Amy stood in the doorway and looked with a jaundiced eye at the film of dust covering everything in the room. It was sparsely furnished, holding little more than the rug and desk. She'd added a small table with a battered but comfortable armchair next to it and an upright chair behind the desk. Everything would have to be moved and dusted. The rug rolled up and the floor vacuumed even the curtains and blind needed attending to.

*   *   *

Her scrutiny took in the fireplace; a heavy sheet of iron blocked its front, preventing any wayward draughts from intruding into the room. She had never tried to move the iron, but now, seeing the outline of white dust around its edges, she pulled at its top, surprised at just how heavy it was. A peep over the rim into the fireplace showed it too had collected its share of dust, and bits of mortar fallen from between the bricks, lay mingled at the bottom of the fireplace.

Replacement of the rotted stumps had caused the mess facing her. True to his word, Tom Floyd had sent his workman out first thing the next morning and the work had begun. An hour later and two more had arrived and the work progressed at an alarmingly speedy and proficient rate, Amy feeding them tea and cakes at appropriate moments so as to keep their energy at its peak. Two days later and the house, once again level, had protested, showing its resentment at such swift and unsubtle handling by showering down dust and mess, causing her extra work.

'You can just wait until tomorrow,' she told

the silent room and walked out, closing the door behind her. The telephone was still not working and she was going to call at Matt's home to check on his cold, but first she would stop at the supermarket and get a few things to make a meal for him. She wanted to make sure he was eating properly, and she considered the idea of staying to share the meal with him. The thought sent a ripple of pleasure through her as she reached for her jacket and car keys and left the house.

'Hello there, Girlie.' Amy stiffened at the form of address coming from behind her as she left the supermarket laden with plastic bags of groceries. She craned her neck around and saw Alec Kander watching her, his usual aggravating grin pulling his mouth sideways.

First Missy and now Girlie. She shoved her irritation to the back of her mind. 'Mr. Kander,' she said pleasantly. 'Mr. Kander, would you have any knowledge of William Tunney building a fireplace at the house?'

Eyes framed by a network of wrinkles snapped at her. 'A fireplace? What would I know about Tunney's fireplace? I had more things on my mind back then than old Tunney and whether or not he had a fireplace. What do you want to know about that for anyway?'

Amy's cheeks flamed at his tone. 'Sorry I bothered you. It's really not important.' She lifted her chin in the air and walked away from him. 'Cantankerous old sod,' she fumed beneath her breath, then realised with a jolt that she was heading in the opposite direction to where she had left her car. Cross and embarrassed she turned into the nearest shop on the pretext of needing something before emerging and this time proceeding on the correct bearing, hoping no-one had wondered why she had been browsing in a shop specialising in erotica.

*   *   *

'Flowers.' Matt eyed the bunch clasped in Amy's hand with some surprise. 'Don't think anyone's ever brought flowers before,' he said, bending to relieve her of the two plastic shopping bags gripped in her other hand. 'I hope your intentions are honourable?' His eyebrows danced cheekily.

She flushed, thinking uncomfortably of the last place she'd been in before here, and returned his laugh, hoping he wouldn't notice the heat she felt rise along her throat. 'Don't be brazen.' She tossed the words across her shoulder as she walked past him into the house. 'I thought they might brighten the place up a bit.' She looked about her at the neutral coloured walls and furniture, and decided the bright gold of the spring daffodils had been a good choice.

Matt was looking much improved, despite a slight huskiness that still lingered when he spoke. He was wearing jeans and a grey jumper with the dark blue collar of his shirt turned out over it. It accented the darkness of his hair and eyes, and the sudden smile he gave her set her heart thumping against her ribs hard enough, she was sure, for him to notice.

Abruptly turning about face Amy walked into the kitchen and began opening cupboard doors, searching for a vase for the flowers, finally settling on a cream jug, and waiting for her breath to return to normal.

Matt placed the bags of groceries on the table and began to unpack them while Amy set about preparing pasta for their meal. Checking under steaming saucepan lids that all was going well she turned her attention to the salad items while Matt got out glasses and poured red wine into them.

Considering his share of the meal preparation done, Matt slouched back on a kitchen chair, glass in hand, and watched as Amy deftly mixed the salad ingredients in a glass bowl before placing it in the refrigerator to wait until the pasta was ready to be eaten. He hadn't missed her faint colouring at his greeting remarks nor her apparently urgent need to find a receptacle for the flowers. Unaware of the major cause of her discomfort, his hopes rose again. His mind had replayed the remarks made by Peter Grant over and over again. Amy had refused to let him spend the night at her place, but he thought he understood at least some of her emotions.

He watched from his comfortable perch while she worked, the sleeves of her soft white woollen jumper pulled above her elbows, pausing occasionally to sip from her glass. Stray tendrils of hair, escaped from their confinement, danced enticingly at the back of her neck, and it was all he could do to restrain himself from reaching out to tuck back the curl that jiggled pertly in front of one ear.

As though sensing his appraisal, Amy raised her head and looked at him across the small mound of torn lettuce leaves before lowering her eyes and resuming her work. No word or sign was exchanged, but Matt settled back on his seat, satisfied with what he had glimpsed in her eyes.

*   *   *

Amy wasn't in Willoughby either. Anger and frustration mingled in Max Harrelson's pale blue eyes as he pressed his foot down on the accelerator of his car. The sudden surge of power made the vehicle swerve dangerously and barely missed clipping the front of a motor-car as it emerged from a parking bay further along the street.

He'd not expected to find Amy straight away, but the longer the search continued the more his patience frayed, and Amy would be made to pay for it.

Approaching the end of the street, he stretched his neck in order to see more clearly that the direction he was taking was the one pointed to by the signpost. Yes. He was heading towards Bingurra.

CHAPTER SIXTEEN

Her car stubbornly refusing to start, Amy had donned her joggers and, giving herself ample time, walked to school. She took the long way around, enjoying the crisp air and the blue and gold of the young day. She entered the school grounds through the narrow gate set in the high wire fence at the rear of the school. Her planned visit to the cemetery later in the day would have to be postponed.

Libby listened to Amy's grumbling at lunchtime while she drove her to the nearest garage. The telephone lines, despite all assurances, were as yet still waiting to be reconnected and the appeal for assistance for her car had to be made in person.

'Is it important to go out to the cemetery today? Won't tomorrow do?'

'Oh, yes, of course it will,' Amy said, grimacing at her own compulsiveness. 'It's just that I'd had my mind made up to look for Gladys' grave. I heard them again last night, Libby. I have to sort this out as soon as possible.'

'You could always move,' Libby said in neutral tones. 'I'm sure Matt wouldn't mind sharing his place with you.' And wondered in the following silence if she had gone too far.

'No,' Amy eventually spoke, firmly but with no trace of being offended. 'It's not a matter of moving out, Libby. I want to find out what happened to Georgie, or at least see if I can discover some way of soothing these poor souls. I keep thinking of that little boy being lost and alone and frightened.'

Libby deftly spun her car around the corner and slowed down as they neared the garage. 'Take my car,' she said, not looking at Amy but keeping her eyes on the approach to the garage door where a litter of discarded metal bits and pieces cluttered the entrance. 'Drop me off at home and go on in my car. Okay?' She applied the brakes and switched off the engine while Amy explained her predicament to the mechanic.

*   *   *

Amy had taken advantage of Libby's offer and in the late afternoon she stood head lowered, as she stared pensively at the grave of William and Lucy Tunney, and the plaque with Georgie's engraved name on it, still lying where she had placed it at the base of his grandparent's headstone. She knelt and

125

placed a small bunch of daisies and fern against the memorial stone. 'Poor little boy,' she whispered. 'What ever happened to you, I wonder.'

The voices had disturbed her again last night, and again she heard the sound of sobbing close by the French doors. Absently her fingers traced the outline of the small piece of granite while her memory replayed last night's sounds. The sobbing bore no trace of the distraught voices calling for the child. Rather its sound was one of utter despair. Her fingers pressed harder against the letters carved on the stone. Gladys. She drew sharp breath. *Could it be? Was that where she she had left her child when her parents had refused her succour? Against the French doors? Had she laid the baby there, her heart breaking with the agony of it?*

The thought of Gladys strong in her mind Amy left the graveside, her eyes roving the perimeter of the small cemetery, seeking some clue as to where the distressed woman would have been buried. Not in these consecrated grounds, she knew, but where else?

Slowly she walked the boundary fence unsure of what it was she sought. The sun shone hot on her bare head and she felt beads of perspiration forming around her hairline. Soon the rest of her body began to feel uncomfortably warm and she removed her jacket and hooking it on one finger slung

126

it across her shoulder as she prowled, her head on a swivel, searching for a clue, something to point her in the right direction.

On an outer side of the wall and close by the far corner of the cemetery's rear wall there grew a pine tree. Wide and high it leaned with its top tilted sociably towards the graves within the cemetery's boundaries. Drawing closer Amy could see a gap in the dry-stone wall where the stones had broken away and lay tumbled nearby. Cautiously she stepped through the space and stood beneath the tree's dark green branches, feeling the cushion of pine needles polished and slippery beneath her feet. She was on the edge of the bush and could see where most of the wattle trees had finished blooming but the new growth on the gum trees caught the late glow of the sun and gleamed fiery red at their tips. The scrub at their base gave sanctuary to the lizards and insects that rustled unseen. *Snakes too?* She shuddered at the thought.

Amy pulled her gaze back from contemplation of possible nasties lurking in the undergrowth to her immediate surroundings and stepped around the generous, rough trunk of the pine to peer around the corner of the wall. She saw three slight but still detectable mounds almost flattened by time and long untended. Grass and weeds sprawled rampantly across them but they were unmistakably graves.

Catching her breath she approached the forlorn sight. *Who were they, these three who have evidently been considered beyond the pale, too unworthy to be interred with the rest of their mortal fellows? Suicides? Probably, poor things.* She shrugged. *I wonder if Gladys is buried in one of them.* 'You must be here Gladys,' Amy said out loud, 'but which one is yours?' Nothing indicated who might be buried in any of the forgotten graves, but she was certain one of the neglected sites held the remains of Gladys Tunney.

Sighing she retraced her steps back through the broken wall and setting her feet on an overgrown path, made her way towards the front gate, all the time conscious of the tears that threatened to spill down her cheeks at the tragedy of it all. She started the car and drove back into town and on to Libby's place.

*   *   *

Her evening meal finished and her few dishes washed and dried, Amy began on her preparations for the next day's work, pulling out the ironing board and sorting out her clothes, but her mind refused to relax, its thoughts on the graves she had found by the cemetery wall. 'Good one Amy,' she suddenly snorted and stared in dismay at the large orange-brown outline of the iron against the white of her shirt spread over the ironing

128

board. She removed the offending item of clothing and rummaged in the cane basket for something else suitable for tomorrow's wear. Briskly she pressed the dark blue shirt before switching the iron off, leaving the rest of her laundry to sit in the basket. She then gathered up a brush, dustpan and dusting cloth and took herself into the room on which she had so firmly closed the door the day before.

Where to begin? She contemplated the scene before her. Placing her work utensils on the floor she moved the desk chair across to the window. Carefully she stood on the chair, obliged to raise up on tip-toe to reach the curtain rod and lift it from its brackets. She let the curtains fall to the floor, raising a soft cloud of dust that tickled her nose, then leaned sideways to prise the blind from its sockets. Both these items, she decided, could wait her further ministrations in the laundry.

The chair back in its position at the desk, Amy crossed to the fireplace and grasping the heavy iron screen in both hands, dragged it to one side and let it rest against the wall, leaving the dank smelling fireplace open and ready for her attention. Brush in hand she knelt and began sweeping the coarse white grit on to her dustpan, trying not to sneeze and scatter the finer particles all over the place. Job completed and herself sprinkled with a fine greyish coating of dust, Amy looked at the gaps left between the brickwork and felt cold air, drawn up from under the house blowing into the room.

She sat back on her heels and studied the haphazard arrangement of the brick and stone fireplace. 'You were no bricklayer, William, that's for sure,' she said to the smoke and soot stained area. She got up to take the carefully collected mess outside to the rubbish bin.

*　　　*　　　*

Her progress through the kitchen was halted when a stream of sunlight shone on the dustpan drawing her attention to part of the debris lying there. Moving to the sink she deposited her load on the bench and gently began separating the larger pieces of crumbled mortar, her eyes squinting with concentration. Selecting several of the pieces she carefully placed them on a tissue pulled from the box near to hand and stood still, looking down, feeling her heart fluttering and her head beginning to throb. She swore softly under her breath because it was late and her telephone was still not working.

*　　　*　　　*

At the top end of the road, his car pulled to the side, Max Harrelson studied a map, and every now and then raised his eyes to scan the knot of people gathered at the gateway.

Some passed the cluster and entered the house others worked their way out to the footpath and their waiting cars, parked in front of, and behind the police car sitting directly outside the premises.

He had taken up his usual watching brief on the Bingurra High School the day before, but failed to see Amy, and was almost tempted to give up and move on to the next town, unaware that, temporarily minus her car she had, comfortably shod, cheerfully, and oblivious of any danger, completely circled the area where he waited and watched.

His expedition was turning out to be more expensive than he'd reckoned on, and he would soon have to consider alternatives for earning more money, but loath to break his routine, he'd returned the following morning and had his reward when Amy drove in through the school gates.

A mixture of emotions flooded through his being and he'd had to exert strong self-discipline to remain where he was and simply watch, careful not to do anything to draw attention to himself. When he heard the school siren sound and saw everyone disappear indoors, he drove through the town and out to the Bingurra reservoir. There he filled in time walking the reservoir's shores and feeding the remains of his lunch to the ducks gathered at the water's edge.

Max returned to his post well before school

131

was dismissed for the day, and as unobtrusively as possible, followed his quarry home, parking at the far end of the road, planning his next move and surprised when cars, including a police vehicle, began assembling at Amy's house.

For icy, heart-stopping minutes he feared he had been discovered and sat, the motor running and his foot poised above the accelerator ready to gun the engine and take off should anyone begin to approach him. No-one paid him the slightest interest and he relaxed, but wary of staying too long, he soon drove off, a smile flickering at the edges of his mouth. He had found her. When the fuss at her house, whatever it was, had died down, he would take Amy back home. Excitement surged through his veins. Soon she would be his again and back where she belonged.

His car parked outside the room he'd rented at the motel on the outskirts of town and his few things collected from his room, Max made his way to the office and paid his bill, keeping his profile as casual and unconcerned as possible. He would roll himself in his sleeping bag and sleep in the car for tonight. When the hue and cry was raised over Amy's disappearance, it would be best if there were no record of anyone checking out of a motel the same day.

CHAPTER SEVENTEEN

The humidity in Brisbane was high. It had rained during the day, a warm rain reminding people that they were approaching the tropical wet season. Greg Stanforth walked into the bar of 'The Feathers' hotel squinting a little until his eyes adjusted to the semi-gloom after the bright outside light.

'Greg Stanforth?' The man Greg recognised as Peter Grant left the bar and walked towards him.

'Peter.' The men shook hands. 'Good of you to meet me,' Greg said.

'No worries. I just hope I haven't caused anyone any trouble.' Peter's eyes showed concern. 'Let's sit over there,' he pointed to a vacant table, 'I'll get a couple of beers.'

'Thanks.' Greg nodded his appreciation.

'Now.' Peter settled himself at the table.

'Yes,' Greg sighed. 'It's about Amy McKenzie, as I mentioned over the 'phone. I'm not too sure how to put this,' his cheeks crinkled, 'but you'll be aware by now that Amy doesn't want Max Harrelson to know where she is and why.'

'Yeah, I know. Damn shame what that bastard did to her. She's a really nice girl. Didn't deserve any of it.' He paused. 'Not that I approve of any woman being bashed,

133

you understand,' he looked quickly at Greg, 'but Amy of all people and the harassment afterwards, I dunno.' He shook his head. 'Anyway, Greg, you can be certain I haven't mentioned anything about Amy to anyone, apart from that night. I guess it was sheer good luck it was you and not someone who'd repeat the yarn, eh?'

'I guess.' Greg nodded.

'I haven't even been in touch with Matt, so there's no way his address could be picked up even that way.'

'So it all seems okay then,' Greg said relieved, 'but I thought I'd better double check with you—you see Harrelson's disappeared and we can't find any trace of him'

'Probably just cleared off for a while.' Peter shrugged. 'Might even be gone for good.'

'Possibly, but I'd like to know for sure where he is. Still if we're the only ones here that know where Amy is she's pretty safe.'

'I'd reckon so. Another beer?'

'Just the one before I leave.' Greg grinned and the two men sat back for a comfortable half hour before Greg left to return to Sarah. Peter Grant had another beer before he too made his way out of the hotel.

'Not good enough,' Sarah told her husband when he reported on his meeting with Peter Grant. 'It's still too uncertain. Greg. If Max finds Amy he'll kill her. I just know it.'

'You could be right.' He chewed

134

thoughtfully on the inside of his cheek. 'It's the fact we don't know where he's gone that's the worry.'

'Try the telephone again,' Sarah urged him.

Greg mopped his face with his handkerchief, the telephone receiver in his other hand slippery with sweat as he replaced it in its cradle.

'Well?' Sarah eyed him anxiously.

'Nothing.' He waved his arms, frustrated. 'They still haven't repaired all the lines down there yet. Reckon it'll be another day before we can get through.'

'What about the police?'

'Police?' Greg twisted himself around the better to see his wife, his eyes wide and forehead wrinkled. 'What could we tell the police? Max Harrelson's gone away, we don't know when, where, why or how.' He ran a hand through his hair, leaving its light brown curls askew.

'Tell them we're worried about Amy. They'll have Max's record there. Ask them if they'll get someone in Bingurra just to check if she's all right. It's reasonable, Greg,' she pleaded, arms folded across her stomach as though in pain.

Greg let out his breath on a long sigh before succumbing to her plea. 'Okay, I'll try.' He patted his pockets, listening for the clink of keys. 'Be better to see them in person than try to explain over the telephone. Come on.' He beckoned to Sarah to precede him, closing the door behind him with a quiet click.

Together they presented themselves at their local Police Station, surprised and pleased at the attention with which their story was heard.

'I remember him,' one policeman said, his face going hard, leaving no doubts as to his opinion of Max Harrelson.

'We'll get them to check.' The police promised of their counterparts down south, and the couple left feeling easier in their minds.

Three hours later their telephone rang. 'There's no need to worry, Mr. Stanforth,' the same policeman told Greg. 'We've been in touch with Bingurra and they tell me they've just returned from Miss McKenzie's place. Apparently some bones were found beneath an old fireplace there and the boys have been out to inspect the area. Your friend is perfectly all right.'

Greg squeezed his wife's shoulders then headed for the refrigerator in search of two cold beers relief plainly reflected on both of their faces.

Old bones? Sarah's mind raised its eyes heaven-wards. Trust Amy. But still, she resolved, she would telephone Amy as soon as the lines were restored. Just to be extra certain that all was well.

*   *   *

'How on earth did he get there, if they are Georgie's bones that is. Come to that, how would any human bones get into such a place?' Libby was agog, her bottom lip sagging with astonishment.

Amy shook her head making her curls bounce with a pertness she certainly was not feeling. She had spent a restless night after the fuss had died down and people had gone, leaving her alone with Matt, who had insisted on returning the favour and preparing a meal for the both of them, and then lingering on until he saw she was in danger of falling asleep in her chair.

Unsure of her next step and uncertain of what she had found, Amy had carefully transported the items folded inside the tissue and placed in a small cardboard box, to school with her the following day. There she'd made her way to the main office building and sought an interview with Sid Dacre.

'They certainly look like bones,' he said. 'But whether or not they're human, I just couldn't say. I'd more than likely think they belong to some sort of animal. A cat or a possum, especially when you consider where you found them.' He peered over his half-spectacles at Amy's troubled face. She had told him of Tom Floyd's information concerning the construction of the chimney, and her concern as to the identity of the fragile pieces

137

nestled in the tissue.

'I think they're finger bones, little finger bones.' She set her lips in a line.

'But Amy. Think of it girl. Think where you found them. It's impossible!'

'I know. I know all that,' she said.

Two vertical lines creased his broad forehead. 'Are you considering that perhaps there may have been foul play involved?'

'No. Never.' She blanched with shock. 'But still, I'll take then to the Police Station at lunchtime. They might be able to help.'

With Matt acting as backup, Amy had caused quite a stir when she presented her find over the counter to the bored and sceptical duty sergeant.

'Bones you say?' He peered at her from beneath bushy eyebrows. 'Possible I suppose.' He shrugged. 'Where did you come across them and what reason do you have for thinking they could be human?'

'I found them when I cleaned out the fireplace at my home.' She flushed realising how pitiful her words sounded.

'What's your name and where do you live?' His expression was definitely one of disbelief.

Amy gave her name and address. 'I think,' she said, 'they could be the bones of a small boy who disappeared a long time ago.' She took care to keep strictly to solid facts and warned Matt with a severe glance to do the same. Files were consulted and the record of the disappearance of George Arthur Tunney was re-read by policemen, unaware until now of Bingurra's greatest mystery. Telephone calls were made and papers filled in, and eventually Amy and Matt found themselves free to return to school. The small cardboard box and its contents were sent for examination at the pathology laboratory in Willoughby.

Word had come back the bones were definitely human, part of a small human hand, and inspection of Amy's fireplace was needed as soon as possible. She'd reached home moments before the first official vehicle arrived, everyone looking very important, trying to conceal the excitement they felt about possibly the most significant police investigation in Bingurra since the disappearance of Georgie Tunney, over sixty years ago.

Two policeman clad in overalls stood, equipment at hand, waiting for the order to begin work. An inspection inside the house of the gaps in the brickwork of the fireplace had decided them to begin work on the outside area of the chimney, on a level with the disintegration of the mortar on the inside.

Carefully the two men began their work, choosing a spot where the chimney was most out of alignment, chipping at the mortar so as not to dislodge the whole thing on to their heads, seeking to make a hole big enough for them to see inside the cavity.

It took only minutes, the crumbling mortar disintegrated at little more than a touch of their heavy tools, the bricks falling away easily into their hands. Amy watched, Matt's arm around her shoulders, while the men created a space large enough for them to shine the light of a powerful torch inside the hole.

The silence was palpable as the policeman with the torch pushed his arm holding the light into the jagged space and followed with his head and shoulders. Unconsciously clutching at Matt's shirt Amy tensed, tightening her grip when she saw the body of the policeman freeze for an instant before withdrawing from the dank chimney and step back, speak to his partner then allow him to take his place and peer inside the blackness. A signal from the second man and a subdued, 'Sir,' from the first policeman brought another policeman, one in plain clothes this time, to their side. Stepping past them he took the proffered torch and peered into the chimney's cavity.

They murmured together, yet another official joined them then the overall-clad policemen resumed their excavating with a care that told Amy what they had found. She clung to Matt as she felt nausea rise in her throat and her legs begin to tremble.

Their faces registering a dozen different emotions as they worked mainly in silence, speaking only when necessary. The men, their faces grim, carefully removed and parcelled

140

their find and took it away.

'Can't tell you much,' the policeman in charge said. 'But it looks as though you were right, Miss McKenzie.' He shook his head and turned from the clouds he saw gathering in her eyes. Ashen faced, she tried to control the tears she felt prickle beneath her lids. 'How . . .' she could not finish the sentence.

'There will have to be an enquiry before we can say anything for sure,' he said, then seeing the white face against the tumble of dark hair, took pity on her and lowered his voice. 'It looks like he's crawled under the house and up into the gap between the bricks, the chimney's so badly built.' He shook his head. It would never be permitted nowadays. 'We found a brick wedged against the side of the head. I'd say it'd been dislodged and fell hitting the little fellow on the head. The top of the skull is broken. A sad business,' he sighed and turned away not wanting to see the tears gathering in Amy's eyes and seeping down her cheeks.

Passively Amy allowed Matt to lead her inside the house, making her sit while he rummaged in her cupboard for some brandy and poured a small amount into a glass for her then set about brewing tea, hot and sweet, and watched while she drank it.

'The locket!' Amy spoke into the silence left after everybody had gone, just herself and Matt remaining at the house.

'What?' He looked at her.

141

'That's where you found the locket. Under the house, near the fireplace.' She shifted in her chair. 'I bet Georgie took it and went under the house to play with it, and panicked when he heard them calling him. Probably knew he'd get into trouble and tucked himself inside the chimney to hide. Who would ever think of looking for him there?' She shivered, imagining how it must have been. 'His movements must've dislodged a brick from higher up and it fell and killed him.' She felt tears threatening again at the thought of the little body entombed all these years, so close to his family and no-one ever knew. She rocked to and fro, arms crossed across her stomach.

CHAPTER EIGHTEEN

Amy closed the door to the room. The outer hole in the chimney had been resealed but she doubted if she would ever be able to bring herself to enter the room again. She thought of transferring the furnishings across the passageway to the smaller room directly behind her own bedroom. 'Maybe later,' she told herself.

A swift peek at the clock sent hcr skittering to the bathroom to shower and change her clothes. Practice was under way for the annual end of year Bingurra High School Concert, and she had promised to help Libby organise the choir. *Of course!* She smiled despite the sorrow she felt about the discovery of the tiny bones in the chimney. She was almost totally bereft of any musical talent, but pleading from Libby, stopping just short of being abject grovelling, plus owing her a favour for the borrowed car, Amy had gingerly agreed to help. It would involve nothing at all onerous Libby had quickly and gratefully assured her. If Amy could just see to it that the choristers were in their correct places, perhaps sort out some of the music etc. She waved a vague hand above her head with a nonchalant air that made Amy instantly suspicious, while she, Libby, would do all the hard work, forming a bunch of mettlesome teenagers into a cohesive, well sounding group.

'Do you mean to say none of these kids have ever performed in a choir before?' Amy demanded, feeling goosy at the very idea of what might lay in store for herself and the would-be choir-mistress.

'No, not really. At least I don't think they have,' Libby said, grinning disarmingly, her green eyes sparkling at the prospect of taming her crew into something outstanding. 'We'll be working with virgin material, so to speak.' She couldn't quite restrain a snicker.

'Libby.' Amy tried to look shocked.

'Sorry.' Libby looked anything but repentant. 'Honestly Amy, all these kids

143

have volunteered for this choir and that's half the battle. I'm positive that with half a chance I can turn them into something really worthwhile, but I need someone to help me to get them organised.'

'Okay. Alright. I said I'd help and I meant it. Who knows, it might even be fun.' Amy had laughed at her friend's anxious expression. Now it was crunch time. Time to see just what she had let herself in for.

Matt would be about somewhere, helping with the scenery for the two-act play the seniors were to present. The ever faithful Jim, uninvolved in any of this so far, would stay in his seat in the auditorium, content to watch his fiancé weave her magic with her charges, and afterwards the four of them would have supper together at the Bill 'n' Coo.

Amy finished readying herself just as Matt's car pulled up before her gate. She shut her front door and skimmed down the short paved path before he could get out of his seat. Neither of them noticed the vehicle sitting well back, but keeping pace with them, and parking opposite the school.

Max Harrelson stared through the tinted windscreen of his car at the backs of Matt and Amy as they walked towards the school hall. The sight of Matt's arm linked with Amy's sent a flood of white hot rage surging through him and his fingers tightened on the steering wheel, his nails digging deep into the leather

144

covering.

He'd watched this morning when Amy drove to school and was waiting at the top end of her road when she returned in the afternoon. He was living rough now, parking his car out of town and crawling into his sleeping bag on the rear seat for the night. He'd not seen any television, but had listened to the car radio and bought a newspaper during the day and read the story of the discovery of human bones. Amy's name was not mentioned, but the story of the disappearance of Georgie Tunney from his grandparent's home so long ago was front-page news, and it was not hard to link it with the bustle he had witnessed at Amy's home the previous day.

He'd had to postpone his immediate plans to take her with him. Not that he didn't have every right to reclaim his wife but he'd had enough of the police breathing down his neck and threatening him with prison if he persisted in annoying her. His lips curled back from his teeth in a sneer at the thought of the police. So here he sat in his car, watching the lights go on and off as she moved about her home, and stiffening with surprise when a car pulled up and Amy had jumped in next to the driver. Curious, he had followed.

The first flush of anger subsiding Max sat quietly, his brain whirling and twisting, examining and discarding one idea after another. Firstly the hustle and bustle concerning the child's bones and now this man that obviously had attached himself to Amy. And he'd not noticed her showing any signs of objecting to the man's closeness either. Things were more complicated than he'd expected. He would have to make alterations to his plans. Perhaps teach them both a lesson while he was at it. He smiled in the dark and his fingers eased their convulsive grip on the wheel. He liked the idea.

*   *   *

'Barbershop Quartet! Just exactly what are you trying to achieve, Libby? A miracle or simply the impossible?' Matt teased good-naturedly.

'It's quite possible,' Libby stoutly defended her idea. 'Maybe not this year,' she conceded, 'but with a bit of work we should have something worthwhile by this time next year. Maybe,' she said slowly as the idea percolated through her brain, 'they'd take better to singing a capella'.

'Not in any year. They'd die at the thought of it. There's no way known you'd get those kids to perform like that.' Matt grinned and rolled his eyes ceiling-wards.

Amy sat back against her seat content to watch the debate with amusement, nodding as each protagonist scored a point and occasionally exchanging knowing grins with Jim, her fellow non-combatant in the group.

146

Matt, as a result of his work in the props department, wore several streaks of white paint in the front of his hair. She thought it gave him a slightly rakish air.

The four of them sat in a booth to the rear of the restaurant, Amy with her back to the wall facing the window overlooking the street with Matt beside her. A clatter of dishes from a near table drew her attention from the conversation and as she watched, a passing figure silhouetted against the lace-curtained windows made her stiffen. *Idiot* she rebuked herself. She would have to stop this habit of imagining she saw Max in every shadow. She turned again to the discussion now fast disintegrating into wild flights of fancy wherein Libby became mentor to a class of exquisite operatic singers.

'Enough.' Firmly Jim called a halt before their mirth became uncontrollable. Rising he placed one hand under Libby's elbow, half pulling her from her seat. 'Time we were gone, I think.' He smiled at his soon to be wife while still gently tugging her from the booth.

'Time we were all on our way,' Matt said, and Amy agreed with him, checking her purse was in her pocket before easing herself out of her seat. They left the restaurant, bidding each other goodnight before separating to go in opposite directions.

Settled in the front seat of Matt's car, Amy felt relaxed and comfortable, allowing him to drive in a silence full of idle content.

'Do you still feel all right about being on your own?' Matt asked the question, his arms tight about her as they stood at her front door. Her hair smelled faintly of green apples, and her mouth was warm and soft when he kissed her. 'I'll be the perfect gentleman,' he grinned down at her in the starlight, wondering if he'd be able to keep his promise.

'I'm fine, Matt. Really.' She kissed the corner of his mouth in appreciation of his thoughtfulness, and felt her stomach turn a somersault at his closeness.

'I just thought that after all the fuss yesterday, and now you've had time for it all to sink in, that you might feel in need of company. Why do you put up with it all?' He burst out in sudden frustration.

'Oh, Matt.' Amy looked up at his dark shadow. 'Lots of reasons I suppose. It's all mixed up inside.' She rested her forehead against his shoulder. 'I was still running when I came here. From myself as much as from Max, I think. Staying here, in the house, was like putting the brakes on. Of refusing to be frightened anymore.' She stirred a little inside his arms. 'Then trying to find out about the Tunneys and Georgie was a catharsis in a way. I feel as though I'm finally finding myself again. Do you understand what I mean?' The pale outline of her features was turned up to him. 'I want to know for sure, and if I let you

148

stay I might never be really certain that I'm my own person again.'

'And when you're sure? Do you think you could share your life again with somebody?' His voice sounded strained. Her perfume, light and warm pervaded his senses.

'Oh yes. I think I'd be only too happy to share with somebody. Matt,' she hesitated then said, 'What about you? Are you ready to share your life with somebody again? You . . . do you . . . I mean,' she stammered not quite knowing how to ask but felt she had to. She had to know if the spirit of his dead finance still lingered. She could not bear the thought of being compared to the dead girl, even subconsciously.

'What?' He rested his chin on her head for a moment. 'Do I still pine for Carmel? Is that it?' Dumbly she nodded not meeting his eyes, afraid of what she might see in them.

'No,' he said. 'For a while, a long time in fact, I thought I'd never get over her death, but it's true, that old saying about time healing. She is a memory, a sweet memory but that's it.' His arms renewed their hold around her, and he kissed her again then released her and waited until she went inside and a light shone through the transom above the front door and then around the edges of her bedroom blind. He returned to his car unaware of the figure further up the road on the opposite side to Amy's house, watching, hidden by the dark

149

overhang of a peppercorn tree, consumed with almost unbearable anger.

*　　　*　　　*

'Drat.' Sarah Stanforth replaced the receiver of her telephone with more vigour than was normally warranted.

'No luck?' Greg stood in the doorway, giving the collar of his shirt a final tug into place and eyeing his wife, who was looking particularly fetching in ankle length black skirt and an almost sheer top embroidered with tiny silver motifs. 'She's probably out, doing the town like we're about to do.' He clicked his fingers and performed a little jig on the spot.

'It's a small country town, Greg, just how much of it do you think there is to "do"?' she asked waspishly.

'For Pete's sake, Sarah. Don't worry. You know the police have checked and she's okay. And I'm sure there are things to do, even in a country town, especially,' he rolled his eyes, 'if this Matt feller Peter Grant mentioned is on the scene. Cheer up, love.' He placed an arm about her waist and deftly spun her about to face their front door. It wouldn't be a late night; they had to be up early in the morning. They were going camping for the weekend.

*　　　*　　　*

150

Amy switched on her bedroom light and waited until she heard the sound of Matt driving away, unconscious of the smile tugging her lips wide and the increased beat of her heart. She really was progressing in leaps and bounds. She could still feel the warm strength of his arms, and she placed her hands on her waist where he had held her. Even the house had a different feel to it. Warmer. More secure. She gave a small laugh. Perhaps it had, now that they had found Georgie, and he would, after a Coronial Inquest, more than likely be interred with his grandparents. Still smiling, she made her way to the bathroom to remove her make-up before tumbling into bed and almost immediate sleep.

Amy woke instantly and completely still, listened. There it was again. She recognised the sound. The French doors were rattling. 'Cut it out, Tunneys. I've done all that can be done. I've found Georgie. There's nothing more to do. There's no need for this anymore,' she muttered turning over and burying her face in her pillow. The noise continued and impatiently she threw the covers off and got out of bed.

Not bothering to switch on the light she padded barefoot from her bed across the passage to the entrance of the front room. Her groping hand found the open doorway in the dark as her senses pricked. She stood rigid, probing the blackness. Seeking out what was different. Then she knew. There was not the usual damp chill in the air that presaged the Tunneys and their disturbances. She frowned. Somebody real had rattled the French doors. Somebody made up of flesh and blood.

The tapping ceased. Amy stood unmoving in the dark for what felt like an age, but heard nothing more. Silently she went on tiptoe from room to room, peering cautiously out of the windows, careful to disturb the curtains and blinds as little as possible. She could see nothing but the black of the night.

She returned to her now cold bed, telling herself the disturbance was more than likely kids playing pranks after hearing the news about Georgie, and thought it a pity parents didn't keep a better eye on their offspring's whereabouts. 'Brats! I'll give them what-for if I see them,' she drowsily promised herself and drifted into sleep, images of Matt Armstrong firmly in her mind.

Max Harrelson heard the creaking of the old floorboards and knew Amy had been disturbed by his tapping. He'd crouched low at the side of the house, sensing as much as hearing her faint movements as she went from room to room. Now he crept from the premises, along the road and around the corner where he had parked his car, and drove away, satisfied with his night's work.

CHAPTER NINETEEN

A feeling of well-being from the previous evening lingered as Matt recalled the feel of Amy in his arms, the taste of her mouth against his. He'd been honest with her question concerning his feelings for Carmel, more honest than he'd realised until that moment.

He indulged himself with a breakfast of waffles lavishly spread with butter and honey. Then held his dishes beneath the tap and ran hot water across them, hearing the hollow gurgle as it emptied down the drainpipe.

Carelessly slamming the door behind him, he walked to his car with long strides and tossed his jacket on to the rear seat before tightening his seat belt and switching on the engine. He contemplated making the half-mile detour that would take him by Amy's place and suggest they drive in together in his car, but a glance at the small clock on the dash told him he was already running late, and she would more than likely have left by now anyway. It was Saturday, but there was a lot of work still to be done to get everything organised for the concert, not all the sets for the play were finished. A working-bee was being held this morning to try and expedite things a bit more. He started the motor and

153

drove happily anticipating his meeting with Amy in mere minutes.

The flick of an eye at the rear vision mirror as he neared the narrow bridge, showed a fast approaching car behind him, its tinted windows giving no clue as to the driver. Lightly he tapped a foot on his brake pedal, hoping the brief flare of red would warn the speedster of the narrowness of the bridge ahead, and felt easier when the car slackened its pace. No Passing. No Overtaking. He read the signs as his front wheels encroached on to the wooden planks and he heard the familiar rumble as the car bumped across them.

Sudden force slammed him forward, his seat belt cut sharply across his chest and his head jerked towards the steering wheel missing it by a fraction. He heard the screech of metal and grabbed wildly at the wheel in front of him, trying to turn it as the car pitched towards the wooden rails of the bridge, hearing loud splintering cracks as the front of his vehicle rammed into the rails. His world went dark.

*   *   *

'There's been an accident at the river bridge.' A member of the working-bee burst into the school hall's small kitchen where the volunteers stood drinking coffee before beginning their appointed chores. His eyes scanned the group, coming to rest on Amy,

154

telling her before he spoke what it was he had to say. 'It's Matt's car,' he said. 'It went through the rails. The ambulance is there,' he jerked the words out, feeling uncomfortable at the way her eyes, suddenly huge in her ashen face, were fixed unblinking on him. 'It didn't go in the river,' he added hastily. 'The front wheels stuck in the bank, skewed, sort of.' His hand sketched a slanting motion. 'The rear wheels are still on the edge of the bridge.'

Amy was halfway out of the room without realising she had moved.

'They'll have taken him to Willoughby,' the messenger said. His fingers plucked at her bare arm. 'I'll take you if you like.'

'No. There's no need. I'm fine. Thanks.' Her head turned towards him, her eyes barely registering his face. Then she was in her car, driving to Willoughby, its hospital and Matt, tight control making her drive more carefully than usual.

Matt would be all right. They'd made her wait, shaking and tense with worry. Liz and Jim had arrived within minutes of her own arrival and sat with her. They spoke seldom and then in hushed tones. For over an hour they waited before a doctor came to give her news. Face pale, eyes anxious she rose at his approach.

Hands thrust into pockets, the doctor grinned cheerfully at her. 'Not too much damage at all, really,' he said. 'A nasty crack on the head, some bad bruising and strains to his chest, arms and shoulders, but really, very, very lucky. The air-bag saved him from a lot worse damage and had the car gone right over the bridge and down into the river, well.' He shrugged, took his hands out of his pockets. 'Your friend is still groggy, slightly concussed,' he told her. 'We're going to keep him here overnight, best to have no visitors just yet.' He smiled with certain sympathy.

'Can I see him please? Just for a short while?' she pleaded.

'Sorry, no.' The doctor shook his head.

'How did it happen?' Amy asked anxiously.

'We're really not sure yet. It's possible another car was involved.' His eyes flicked past her recognising someone behind her. 'Excuse me,' he said and with a reassuring nod, left her to go and speak to the large, grey-haired policeman who'd caught his attention.

Amy waited until the doctor and the policeman ended their conversation then hurried to catch the officer before he disappeared into his vehicle and drove off.

'Your boyfriend is he?' The large policeman looked down from his six foot four inches.

'Yes.' Amy nodded not taking time to ponder the question. 'What can you tell me? Was another car involved? Did Matt's car skid on oil or something?' She waited her eyes fixed on his face.

'Didn't skid, not as far as I could tell, but

there are signs of dark blue paint on the rear of your friend's motor.'

Amy caught her breath. 'Paint? He was rammed then? Deliberately?'

The officer shrugged. 'Not sure yet, could've been someone in a hurry and not realised how narrow the bridge is. The main thing is, your boyfriend is okay. A bit sore and sorry for himself for a while but he'll be fine the doc said.'

'Yes.' Amy nodded. 'Yes, thank you.' She gave a small smile and left to go to her own car.

All the way home Amy puzzled over the accident. Another car? Couldn't the damn fools read, or were they speeding and hadn't seen the signs as it came from behind, trying to pass and forced him over the side. Anger shook her at the carelessness of the other driver and the very real possibility of Matt having been killed or maimed for life.

Amy let her car roll to a standstill at the side of the house, acknowledged the farewell toot of Jim's car as he and Libby departed after following her home. She switched the motor off and sat in the silence, aware of her still shaking limbs. In contrast, her face felt numb, although she knew her lower lip and chin were beginning to tremble, and her heart fluttered against her ribs. Shock was overtaking the control she had exerted for the last few hours. She looked around at the grass-covered yard now liberally sprinkled with the yellowing leaves left behind by the spent daffodils and jonquils, and the carpet of yellow daisies that had taken their place. The willows were in full leaf now, their long green fronds sweeping the ground in places. A cup of coffee, strong and black was what she needed. The sun was warm and she would take her drink out to her now favourite spot beneath the willows and drink it there. She would return to the hospital this evening and with luck, Matt would be awake and able to tell her what had happened. She shivered again at the thought of how easily the accident could have been fatal.

Her key in hand she swung the wire door open. Something soft squelched beneath her feet. She shifted her glance downwards. A bunch of flowers lay on the doorstep, their stems now under her feet. The flower heads in a neat pile at the opposite end of the step. Her body went cold and she found it hard to breathe. Max!

*   *   *

Coffee cup clasped between both hands and her breathing normal once more, Amy derided her panic of a short while before. She had forgotten her intention of sitting outside under the tree, was instead seated at her kitchen table and reassured by the feel of its solid timber and the sturdy surety of the chair

158

beneath her.

So much for her brave words of, was it only last night? The slightest thing out of the ordinary and she was on the verge of hysteria.

Back up there girl. Indignation stiffened her. *You've coped with a haunted house haven't you? Even done detective work trying to discover what happened to Georgie. That the actual discovery of his tiny skeleton was due purely to the incidence of the house being re-stumped doesn't lessen the fact of your efforts and dogged determination not to be frightened off the same as every other tenant this house has had. You're not lacking in courage, so why the mad panic at a handful of beheaded flowers lying on the doorstep? As for the sounds you heard last night. It was most likely someone's idea of a joke after the finding of Georgie's little bones. Sick!*

Slowly but surely Amy convinced herself her panic was merely a form of shock reaction over Matt's accident, but just in case . . . She refilled her coffee cup and walked to the telephone and dialled a number, listening until it rang out. Greg and Sarah Stanforth were not at home.

*   *   *

'The police were right then? You really were rammed? On purpose! What an idiot, how could they be so stupid.' Aghast, Amy stared at Matt, trying to take in his words. He looked

159

awful. A large multi-coloured swelling stood out over one eye and spread down the side of his face, his eye was bloodshot and half closed. She could just see, beneath the opening of his pyjama jacket, angry red welts running across his chest where his seatbelt had prevented him from catapulting through the windscreen, and he winced with the pain of strained shoulder muscles. Still, he had been unbelievably fortunate to escape so lightly. Belatedly, Amy recalled the scene of Matt's accident was the same bridge where the Flemings had met their death the night they fled, unable to share the same house as the Tunneys any longer.

Matt began to nod his head in agreement at her exclamation, winced and thought better of it and gave vocal reply. 'The idiot could have killed us both.' He went on to repeat what he'd told the policeman, about the speeding car behind him and his effort to alert the driver to the narrow bridge.

'Idiot. Maniac.' Fright and anger made her voice hard. 'I hope they throw the book at him.'

'First they have to catch him,' Matt's tone was dry.

'You've no idea who it was?'

'The car was a blue Nissan about ten years old; its windows were tinted. That's all I noticed.' He managed a tired smile. 'I was running late.'

She stroked his hand, compassion for him

160

replacing her anger at the unknown assailant. She sat quietly by his bed until he slept. *Was it? Could it possibly have been Max?* Fear shimmied down her spine.

*   *   *

In the dark of the night Max Harrelson huddled inside his sleeping bag on the back seat of his car. The day had been warm but now the evening was chilly.

The crash this morning was an impulse. He'd watched the quartet leave the school last evening, had followed discreetly when they drove into town. Unable to resist, he had walked slowly past the restaurant, saw them inside under the bright lights seated in a booth at the rear of the room. Saw the man next to Amy with his arm along the padded back of the seat behind her, his fingers possessively brushing against her sleeve. Just as he'd passed, Amy had lifted her head, and for a fleeting second seemed to look right at him.

He'd trailed behind again when the man took Amy home, watched the sickening scene of them kissing then followed the bright red wink of rear lights to where the man lived.

He'd returned in the early morning, watching, waiting to get a good look at his opposition, and then, when the man quick-stepped to his car and drove off in obvious hurry Max followed without thought, anxious not to lose him.

He'd experienced a flare of anger at the warning when the man's stoplights had flickered at him. The warning signs posted at the bridge's end became a clear invitation. He'd pushed his foot down on the accelerator and positioned his car so that his outside wheel was in line with the rear inside wheel of the car in front. He had rammed the vehicle hard, turning his steering wheel so as to allow himself to bounce back into the centre of the bridge and make a clear getaway across to the other side. A fast look in his rear vision mirror and he saw the car smash into the side railings and its nose dip dangerously downwards, then he was around the bend and the scene was cut from his view.

Steadily Max circled the town until he reached the outskirts where he parked well out of sight of any passer-by. An examination of his car showed damage to the front, but nothing extensive enough to draw a lot of unwanted attention.

Avidly he listened to a report of the accident on his car radio. He was pleased to have caused injury to the man and put him in hospital for a time. He would have been even happier had the man died. It wasn't beyond the realms of possibility that such a thing could be arranged. He smiled, liking the idea.

It was quite dark now, but he would wait a while yet, until the residents of this quiet little country town had mostly gone to sleep, then he would pay Amy another visit. He laughed at the thought and there was in the sound of it, a pitch that would unsettle anyone who heard.

Amy regarded her reflection in the mirror and pulled a face at it. Her usual healthy glow had faded leaving her looking drawn; there were dark blue shadows beneath her eyes and frown marks between her brows. She discarded the red shirt in her hands for the softer apricot tee-shirt that reflected a warmer lustre upwards towards her face. She pulled it on over her head and hitched up her jeans.

She hadn't slept much last night and felt its deprivation this morning, plus, try as she might, she could not rid herself of the nameless unease that persisted in lurking at the back of her mind. She had dialled the Queensland number again last night when she arrived home from the hospital. Again she had listened until the dial tone rang out.

She had gone from room to room, checking that all windows and doors were securely locked, chiding herself but unable to ignore the compulsion urging her onwards. She had lain in the dark, listening, until her eyelids closed from sheer exhaustion. Only once did she hear anything out of the ordinary. A muffled noise accompanied by a dull thud from the rear of the house, then silence. She had made her way to the kitchen in the dark to peer bleary-eyed through the kitchen window but saw nothing. There was no moon to give light and she had been unable to distinguish any movement in the dark.

She'd returned to bed, touching the heavy torch beneath her pillow, reassuring herself that it was still there. She would try telephoning Greg and Sarah again during the day. It would be too much of a coincidence for Max to turn up here right now, but she had to satisfy her niggling unease and be certain that he was still in Queensland. Greg and Sarah would not laugh at her, she knew. They had been too close to the events of the past. They knew full well what Max could be like. The image of the beheaded flowers on her doorstep still haunted her.

Hair pulled back and secured with a heavy tortoiseshell clip, Amy was ready. She opened the far end drawer of the kitchen dresser and pushing her hand to the rear, pulled out a small mother of pearl penknife given to her by her grandfather when she was ten years old. She opened the tiny knife and checked the small but very sharp blade, then closed it again and tucked it inside her bra, the nacre quickly warming against her flesh. It was not much in the way of protection should she need any, and most probably would be frowned upon by the police if they knew, but it made her feel more secure.

Grabbing up her bag she locked the door behind her and walked to her car, her eyes scanning anywhere that could be used for possible concealment. She was on her way to pick Matt up from the hospital and take him to his home.

*   *   *

Max pulled the elastic bandage firm about his ankle, cursing as pain shot up his leg. There was an unexpected dip in the yard at Amy's house. One he'd not seen in the dark, and he had tripped, falling heavily and twisting his ankle.

He saw the faint blur of her face as she peered from the kitchen window, and had stayed flat and unmoving on the ground until he was sure she was gone before rising to limp awkwardly back to his car.

The strain didn't appear to be too severe, but he used the bandage from the first-aid kit he kept in the glove box as a precaution, bound and rested for the day should see the ankle strong enough to support him without too much bother by this evening. It would be tonight, he decided, that he and Amy would be reunited.

CHAPTER TWENTY

'Hello.' Amy brushed a brief kiss against Matt's cheek, aware of the attending nurse's gaze and careful not to touch his face where bruising now extended to cover the side of his face from brow to jawline.

'Hi,' Matt greeted her with a lopsided grin that made her heart lurch, and she wanted to clutch him to herself in a fierce embrace.

'Ready?' Amy waited while he cast a final glance around satisfying himself that he'd not forgotten anything. The effort of getting into his shirt and buttoning it across the bruising and tender muscles of his chest and shoulders forced Matt to allow the nurse to complete the job. Amy brushed to one side had to be content to hold his jacket over one arm while her other hand gripped the small bag containing his toiletries.

'Ready.' He fell into step beside her, the hovering nurse leaving them at the Ward entrance, the demarcation of her boundary.

Amy settled Matt into the front seat of her car, carefully wadding a soft towel where his seat belt would diagonally cross his bruised chest. They travelled mostly in silence, the warm sun and the green of the countryside soothing them. Matt relaxed, enjoying the sensation of allowing himself to be chauffeured, Amy debating whether or not to tell him of her worries concerning Max. She had, bit by bit, told him of her life with Max. Not all of it, not by any means, but enough. He understood her reluctance, her wish to begin fresh, with no-one knowing of her marital traumas. 'It clouds people's perceptions, consciously or unconsciously,' she'd told him, clouds at the back of her eyes when she looked at him. He had kissed her and grinned wickedly down at her. 'My perceptions of you are very clear, there's not a cloud in sight.' She had laughed, pleased.

*   *   *

She drummed her fingertips softly on the steering wheel. 'So, do you know yet if the police have any idea of who it was ran you off the bridge?' she asked tentatively beginning to feel her way.

'Tony Semmens called by early this morning,' Matt said, naming one of Bingurra's two policemen. 'They found tyre tracks leading out of town. He reckons the damn idiot kept right on going.' He let his anger momentarily dispel his misery. Gingerly he rubbed one hand over his chest, aching despite Amy's efforts to keep to the smooth parts of the roadway.

'Coward,' Amy muttered. 'He probably panicked and then was too gutless to come back and own up to what he did.' She snorted in disgust then sighed. 'Oh. Well, I guess that'll be the end of that, then.' She decided she wouldn't tell Matt her worries after all. If the tyre tracks led out of town, then it was almost certain that it wasn't Max. Besides, she reasoned, Max could not be aware that Matt was of any interest in her life. There'd be no cause to attack him. She'd been right the first time, it was just some rat-bag, kids probably, making noises and leaving the beheaded flowers at her place because of the discovery of Georgie. Matt's accident was simply a coincidence. She would stop being neurotic and put the little penknife back in its drawer when she got home.

'I did some grocery shopping early on, thought we'd have omelette and salad for lunch, and I've got other stuff to put in your freezer to keep you going for a while.' She turned her car smartly into Matt's driveway and parked in front of his door.

True to her word, Amy made omelette and salad for their lunch, with crusty bread rolls warmed in the oven, and a half bottle of wine to wash it all down. The rest of the afternoon they spent comfortably on the couch, eyes fixed on the television set, watching an old movie.

It was getting on for nine o'clock when Amy left Matt's house. She drove homewards contentedly in the rapidly deepening twilight. She had fussed a little over Matt before leaving, establishing he was capable of getting himself settled for the night, much to his amusement and secret delight. His invitation to Amy to stay and make certain he was comfortable had been firmly if somewhat reluctantly refused.

'There's concert practice again tomorrow evening, so I won't be here until late. If it's too late, say after ten, I won't come. I'll telephone in the morning anyway just to make sure you've survived the night.' She flashed a quick smile in his direction.

'I'll be fine, don't worry about it,' he told her. He had noticed the way her fingers tapped the steering wheel during their journey home, the tense set of her shoulders. Amy had something on her mind beside himself and he wondered when she would get around to telling him.

CHAPTER TWENTY-ONE

Amy let herself inside the house and flicked on the light before crossing the room to close the blinds. Twilight had given way to night and stars were beginning to show faintly as the sky deepened its hue. She could hear the brisk song of the crickets down past the willows, giving her promise of a hot day tomorrow.

'Hello, Amy.' Instant cold swept across

169

her and her chest tightened until she could barely breathe. Slowly she turned, her fingers gripping the edge of the sink to steady herself and stop her legs from giving way beneath her.

He stood in the passage doorway to the kitchen. For a moment all she could distinguish was his face, floating pale against the dark background. Gradually, as the blurring of her eyesight cleared, she could make out the rest of his form, dressed in black and blending in with the dark of the unlit area behind him.

'Max.' Her voice cracked as she fought down rising nausea. She must keep her voice as calm as possible and hope he hadn't noticed its tremor.

'The very same.' He emerged fully into the kitchen, his pale hair dull and lank and the faint odour of unwashed clothing hanging about him. 'Surprised to see me Sweets?' He enjoyed watching her discomfort, obvious in spite of her endeavour.

'How did you find me, Max, and what do you want?' Fear surged through her but she was pleased to hear the snap she managed to put in her tone despite it.

'You're my wife, Amy.' Max opened his eyes wide, their washed out blue glinting with reflected light, a look of hurt surprise in them. 'I've come to take you home sweetheart.'

'No. I'm not your wife and I'm not going anywhere with you. We are divorced, Max.

You have no right here at all. Now get out. I'll report you for breaking and entering.' Her temper rose. She had lived in fear of this day for a long time, but felt outrage at her carefully restructured life being so rudely disregarded. His utter contempt for anyone's wishes except his own, made her temporarily forget her physical safety and what Max was capable of doing when he felt pushed too far.

'You just love to have those boys in blue hovering about, don't you?' He placed his hands flat on the table and leaned across it, his eyes sparking with anger. 'I saw them running around here the other day.' His lips flattened in a thin line. 'Making yourself into quite a personage in the area, aren't you? Favourite trick of yours, isn't it?' His features twisted into a sneer.

She watched the veins at his temples beginning to stand out, and felt a tremor of apprehension replace her anger. She'd seen Max work himself into tempers like this before, usually with violent results, herself the victim.

'How did you find me?' She repeated her question, hoping to distract him from what she was certain would be his present trend of thought.

'A bloke in a pub.' He laughed, happy at her puzzled expression.

'What? Someone in a pub?' Genuine surprise pitched her voice higher. 'It couldn't

171

have been.' She pulled her eyebrows together. She was certain it couldn't have been Greg who gave her away. She'd bet her life on that. Neither Greg nor Sarah was the type to blab about things. She set her jaw and tried to squash the quaking deep in her stomach. 'I don't believe you. There's nobody in Brisbane that could know where I live.'

''fraid you must, Sweets. Somebody you know mentioned your name to somebody he knows, and was overheard by somebody who knew I'd be interested. See?' And he laughed again, obviously delighted in her confusion and his own cleverness.

The thought darted into her brain with painful sharpness. Matt had met Peter Grant at the reunion. She choked back the bitterness she felt rise in her throat. 'Who was it? Who told you? How did you know to come to Bingurra?' She fired the questions at him, keeping him talking, distracted, while she edged with snail-like slowness along the front of the sink and towards the door, the palms of her hands wet with perspiration now behind her back and flat against the cupboard front. A few more steps and she'd be close enough to make a dash for it.

'That's a no-no.' All signs of good humour gone in a flash, Max sprang forward and slammed his hand against the door. 'Planning to dash off were you?' He turned the key in the door with a vicious twist then grabbed her by

172

the shoulders with both hands, his stale breath gusting across her face as he yelled at her in anger. 'Wouldn't be trying to get away to the boyfriend at all, would you?' His fingers dug deep into her flesh and he shook her, making her head jerk sickeningly to and fro.

'Stop it, Max!' The words came out in ragged gasps. *He knows about Matt.* Fear twisted in her stomach like a rat nibbling at her insides. She felt tears form in her eyes and her nose began to run as the terror of his former torments washed over her once more and coupled with the fear of what his next move might be. She heard harsh grunting noises and realised they came from her own throat as she twisted her body in an effort to break his grip.

With a violent shove Max slammed Amy against the wall and released her arms, only to plunge one hand deep into her mass of hair, twisting its curls around his fingers and pulling her hard towards him until their faces were all but touching.

'I've come to take you home, Amy.' His eyes were cold. 'You've had your little bit of excitement, running away, leading another man on, pretending you were free. You've cost me a lot of time and expense, but I've found you and . . . you . . . will . . . come . . . back . . . with . . . me.' The words were spoken with a clear, cold anger.

'No.' Truly frightened now, her body shuddering at his touch, she tried to push him away, jerking her head away from his face. Frustrated she lashed out with one foot, the toe of her boot catching him on his sore ankle.

His reaction was immediate. He swung his free fist and hit her on the jaw, making no effort to catch her as she crumpled, dragging her hair through his half clenched fingers, letting her unconscious form sag to the floor.

He swore viciously as the pain shot up his leg while he looked at Amy's crumpled body. He paid no heed when the telephone began to ring, letting it ring itself out while he contemplated his next move.

*   *   *

Exasperated, Sarah Stanforth hung up the telephone. Still no answer. She walked into the bedroom and began unpacking her own and Greg's bags. She would try telephoning again in the morning before Amy would have left for school.

*   *   *

Max carried Amy's unconscious form into the front room and using cords from the window drapes tied her to the chair then went to her bathroom and rummaged through her medicine cabinet for something to rub on his ankle. She had packed a solid wallop with her boot, and the pain was shooting up his leg in long hot streaks.

He rubbed the point of impact with salve from her medicine cabinet and wound one of her bandages about the afflicted area. He rechecked that she was not yet stirring and her bindings secure then hobbled into the kitchen and poured a liberal portion of her brandy into a glass and took it and the painkillers he'd taken from the bathroom into her bedroom.

Easing on to the bed and placing a pillow beneath his injured ankle, he swallowed the painkillers and sipped his drink, waiting for the throbbing in his leg to abate, gradually slipping into sleep. His first good sleep in a proper bed in days.

*   *   *

Consciousness returned slowly to Amy. Her world was bleary and tinged with red and black until she was able to keep her eyes open and her brain began to function coherently once more. She was uncomfortably folded into the armchair in the front room. The side of her face ached and her jaw felt stiff where Max had hit her and she panicked for a moment wondering if it was broken. She attempted to ease her posture and found her hands had been tied behind her back, adding to her cramped and uncomfortable position.

She raised her head and listened. The house was silent and through the chinks in the drapes

175

covering the French doors she could see bright starlight. She wondered how long she'd been unconscious. Where was Max? She strained her ears to hear any sound he might make but could detect nothing. There was only silence.

With a struggle she managed to sit herself upright. Her ankles were securely bound, one end of the rope tied to the leg of the heavy chair. Her movements were awkward, and she was aware of something digging into her breast. Her penknife. It still nestled inside her bra, but it may as well have remained in the dresser drawer for all the hope she had of getting hold of it.

She heard the sound and stiffened, listening. The snoring came from her bedroom. A look of incredulousness crossed her face and she began to laugh, hearing in it a note of hysteria.

CHAPTER TWENTY-TWO

Matt was up and dressed early. He'd been awake since first light and decided his muscles would benefit more from his moving about than lying stiff and uncomfortable on a mattress.

He looked at the clock for maybe the tenth time, double-checking with the hands on his wrist watch. Not wanting to examine the niggling disappointment he felt. Amy hadn't telephoned this morning as promised. She would be at school by now, her classes already commenced.

He ran long fingers through his dark hair. He had sensed her unease yesterday, had waited for her to confide in him. When she said nothing he'd let it be, too conscious of his own aches and pains to be fully sensitive to her possible needs, happy to blame his accident for her upset. Perhaps a stroll would help him sort out some of the kinks, mental as well as physical. He pulled the door shut behind him and set off at a slow pace along the gravel road.

'You look awful,' Alec Kander told Matt as the old man's smart, shiny car pulled up beside him. 'Come back to the scene of the crime have you?' The grin wrinkling his weather-beaten skin was anything but sympathetic.

'Good morning.' Matt's greeting was polite but distant. He marvelled at the old devil's knack of getting under everybody's skin.'

'No girlfriend to hold your hand this morning?' Definite sneer here. 'Don't tell me she's ditched you now you've mucked up your looks.' He sniggered.

'Amy has classes this morning, Alec, as I'm sure you well know,' Matt said, gritting his teeth. He really had walked too far. Everything hurt and the thought of the return trip a daunting prospect. He was in no mood to take much more of this rot. If Alec Kander wasn't

177

going to offer him a lift, then he could just be on his way. Find some other poor sod to torment with his snide remarks.

'Dunno about that, laddie,' Alec said baring his yellowed teeth. He was enjoying himself. Thoroughly. 'I just passed her place. Her car's still there, so's the one I saw there last night. Perhaps she doesn't fancy you anymore and has found herself someone else. More appealing in the looks department at least.' He emitted a rusty cackled.

Matt scowled into the face. His ill humour made his injuries hurt even more. Wordlessly he moved around the car and opened the passenger side door and climbed in. 'Drive me home.' It was an order not to be ignored, not even by the irascible Alec Kander.

'Thanks,' Matt said as Alec's car came to a halt outside his house.

'You'd've been jiggered if I hadn't come along. I reckon you thought you were fitter than you are,' Alec commented sourly. 'Better have a bit of a lay down before rushing off to check on young Amy. She wouldn't want you falling into a heap at her feet now, would she?' He stared at the steering wheel. 'Didn't really mean what I said about her ditching you, though you probably deserve it,' he chuckled his usual phlegmy sound.

'Yeah, you're probably right.' Matt screwed up his sore face in what he hoped looked halfway to a friendly grimace. 'About that car though, was there really one there Alec? I'm serious, it could be important.' He waited hoping Alec would sneer and tell him he was easily taken in.

'One there all right,' the old man affirmed. 'Dunno whose it was, but it was there all night I'd say. No-one from around here I don't think. I know pretty well who drives what around here.'

Matt stood up straight and wagged a couple of fingers at Alec as he hobbled inside to his telephone. He would telephone the school first, make sure Amy hadn't been caught with a non-start car again and walked to school. The other car in her yard could be anyone . . . a friend, relation called unexpectedly. His gut however told him otherwise, but before he could dial the number, the phone rang.

'Hello? Hello? Is that Matthew Armstrong?' A female voice asked.

'Yes. Can I help you?' His forehead pleated as he tried to place the voice.

* * *

'My name,' the woman said, is Sarah Standforth. I got you name from Peter Grant . . . I'm a friend of Amy's. Amy McKenzie. I believe you know her.'

'What's this about?' Caution warned Matt not to bc too forthcoming until hc kncw morc of what the telephone call was about.

179

'Umm . . . I've been trying to get in touch with Amy but she's not answering her 'phone, neither last night nor this morning. Would you happen to know where I could get in touch with her? It's rather urgent.'

Apprehension prickled along Matt's spine. 'Right now she should be in class,' he said. 'Is . . . is this to do with her ex by any chance?'

'She's told you about Max?' Sarah queried.

'Yes.' The hair on the back of his neck prickled.

'Well then you're right I'm afraid,' Sarah said. 'Max disappeared a couple of weeks ago and my husband and I don't know where he's gone. From the little we've been able to find out he evidently just threw in his job and took off. I know he most likely has no idea where Amy is, but I thought I'd warn her just in case, and not being able to reach her has me really worried. Uh, Matt, is there any way you can get in touch with her?'

'Not a problem,' Matt assured Sarah, unwilling to tell her about the car Alec Kander saw in Amy's yard last night. 'I'm on my way over there now,' he said, his urge to get to Amy's house suddenly urgent. 'I'll get her to ring you as soon as possible, okay?'

'Thanks,' Sarah replied, relief in her voice. 'I'm probably worrying for nothing, but . . .'

'I understand. 'bye now.' Matt hung up the telephone and hurried outside.

Unheeding of the pain that streaked up his

arms and across his chest and shoulders, Matt thumped the roof of his car again and yet again. The tyres on his green Ford had been slashed. Every one of them.

The tumblers in Matt's head clicked solidly into place concerning Amy's discomfort yesterday over the cause of his accident and his own sudden suspicions about the strange car Alex said he'd seen parked in Amy's yard. It explained why Amy had not answered Sarah's call. Max had found her. But how? Had he somehow found out about Matt's talk with Peter Grant at the reunion? Sweat beaded his forehead at the thought. He'd never forgive himself if Amy came to harm.

The woman, Sarah, had said over the telephone that Max had left Queensland weeks ago. If it was Max's car Alec had seen the night before then he must have already been watching Amy. For how long? He wondered. Hours, days even? How long had it taken him to find her? Had Max followed Amy here then sneaked in and slashed the tyres on Matt's car before heading back to Amy's? Then what? Did he just sit and wait for her to return home? What did he have in mind? His gut twisted.

It had to have been Max who tried to run him off the bridge. Tried to kill him. Matt's head spun and he gripped the back of a chair to steady himself as a wave of vertigo swept over him. Amy was in danger! He must get to

181

her and hope it was not already too late.

*   *   *

Amy squirmed in her chair. She had been stuck in it all night, dozing off and on, waking with a start, her heart thumping, ears straining to catch the sounds of Max as he slept. She struggled with her bonds, succeeding only in chaffing her wrists and ankles. Now her bladder was insisting she visit the toilet.

She shivered as she heard the sounds of Max stirring and waited, her already aching muscles tensing while she listened. She heard him visit the toilet and then its flushing. She heard him move to the kitchen and the sound of the tap being turned on and off and noises, indicating Max was drinking water. She waited for his approach. Finally he stood before her, his back to the French doors, his shape outlined against the thin drapes. Dark and threatening he regarded her, angry that his plans to leave last night had been botched because of her.

'Have a good night's sleep, Pet?' he said, his expression judging her obvious discomfit as punishment for her previous behaviour.

'Untie me, Max. I need to go to the toilet.' The uncomfortable pressure of her bladder made her words short and sharp.

But he merely cocked his head to one side and raised his eyebrows. 'Manners Amy.

Manners.'

'Please, Max. Let me out of the chair. Please.' She eyed him angrily. 'I'm desperate.'

For answer he untied the rope binding her legs to the chair. 'No more smart stuff, Amy,' he warned. 'I'll really have to hurt you if you try that.' He giggled a sound that sickened her, and his fingers pressed deep into her shoulders as he pulled her from the chair. 'What happened to your boyfriend will be a picnic to what I'll do to you if you play up again.' The close-up odour of him was rank, he'd not bothered to take advantage of Amy's bathroom to wash either himself or his clothes. 'You haven't kissed me good-morning, yet.' He bent his head to hers. Repulsed, she took an involuntary step backwards, and received a slap across her face before he held her head tight between his hands and kissed her hard his tongue trying to force its way between her teeth.

'It was you wasn't it?' Amy stared at Max with loathing as he eased his grip on her shoulders. 'You tried to drive Matt off the bridge.'

'The opportunity was there so I took it.' He giggled. 'I saw the way he pawed you at the restaurant,' he sneered, angry colour suffusing his features. 'You looked up just as I walked by. I thought you'd seen me.' He squeezed her shoulder again making her wince with pain.

Her head began to throb. She wanted to

scream and shout, to claw the very skin from his sneering face. Her heart felt as if it was about to stick in her throat and choke her.

'Come on.' Roughly he grabbed her by the arm and they made their way to the bathroom.

'My hands.' She looked at him. 'I can't. Not with them tied behind my back.' Colour flooded her cheeks.

He stared at her, allowing her to see the thoughts clearly running through his mind, as his eyes roamed the length of her body.

'Stop that and untie my hands.' She stood rigid, anger and disgust flaring in her countenance.

'Stand still.' His examination of her changed, this time he was obviously seeking pockets that could hold anything that might pose a threat to him. She waited for him to demand the pocket-knife secreted in her bra. With quick movements he jerked the rope free from one wrist, allowing her to bring her stiffened arms to the front. 'Not so fast.'

She watched in disbelief as he grabbed her wrist with the rope still attached and pulled a thin nylon cord from his pocket, tying one end of it to the rope.

'Better safe than sorry.' He leered at her, and cupping one hand around her chin covered her mouth with his before pulling back and, his fingers digging painfully into her bruised jaw, he gave her head a shake. 'There's nothing in there you can do any damage with, and I'll know if you try anyway.' He released her. 'I'll just hold on to this end.' His voice was complacent as she turned and entered the bathroom.

Dragging as much of the rope as she dared into the room with her, Amy pushed the door as tightly shut as she could manage, jamming the rope tight.

While she sat on the toilet she felt inside her bra and extracted the penknife. Bracing her wrist to keep the cord firm she sawed through the cord then tucked the severed end between her wrist and the rope. She left the blade of the knife exposed and slid it into the palm of her hand, its handle kept in place beneath the edge of her bond, the blade lying snugly between two fingers. 'Ready.' She opened the door and walked into the kitchen.

Max sat at the table, directly below the skylight. 'Some breakfast before we leave, I think, Amy.' He smiled, certain now of his control over her.

She passed the end of the table and walked towards the sink, making sure to keep her bound wrist slightly behind her, watching him from the corner of her eye as he sat back, lulled by the feel of the end of the cord held in his grip. One more step and she was at the end of the bench and close to the door. Fingers outstretched she flung herself forward, turning the key and wrenching the door open before Max, his eyesight dulled by the glare of bright sun from the skylight above, realised what she was about. He sprang after her, leaping the width of the table. Almost, she was through the door when his fingertips clutched the neck of her blouse and heaved her back into the kitchen.

'No,' Amy screamed, lashing out at his face with her fists, the tip of the knife gouging skin from his cheek. 'No.' Her nails scored the other side of his face.

'Bitch.' His backhanded slap knocked her to the floor and stood over her shaking form. 'You'll pay for this Amy, believe me you'll really pay.' Twisting her wrist he dislodged the penknife then held it pressed against her top lip just below her nostrils.

'Don't. Max you have to let me go. This is madness.' Sobbing she tried to scrabble back out of his way until she pressed against the kitchen bench.

'Never.' His pale eyes glittered chips of ice. 'We're going now.' He grabbed her by the shoulder his fingers pressing painfully into her flesh and pulled her to her feet then shoved her towards the door.

Stepping off the doorstep Amy suddenly let her knees buckle and at the lessening of Max's grip she threw herself forward, hearing the fabric of her blouse tear, and then was running across the yard, unseeing of any direction, simply running as far from Max as possible.

Halfway across the yard her flying feet met

the slight dip that presaged the old mine shaft, she stumbled across it and lost her balance. Her left ankle twisted beneath her and she fell, hitting the ground with a thud that knocked the breath from her body. Unable to move, frantic to draw air into her lungs, she watched in misery and fear as Max, seeing her plight, slowed his pursuit and walked towards her, his steps deliberate. Gently he slapped the severed end of the cord against the palm of his hand and the set of his face boded her nothing but pain. A lot of pain.

'Stop. Max you must stop this. Please,' her voice cracked with the effort to speak. 'This is insane, you must stop.' Still he came towards her, his eyes icy, the slapping of the cord against the palm of his hand clear in the morning air.

'You are mine,' he whispered, a cruel smile on his lips.

He reached the edge of the dip she'd tripped on, his eyes glittered like chips of blue ice, blood from the knife cut trickled down his face. Another few paces and he would have her she knew. There'd be no escape this time. This time he would kill her. His eyes still fixed on her in an unblinking stare he took another step and disappeared.

How long she sat there, stunned and disbelieving, Amy didn't know. Trying to even out her breathing she gradually left her sitting position and rolled onto her stomach, then plucked up courage to inch her way forward bit by bit until she could gaze down into deep dark space. Shock threatening to overwhelm her she scrabbled backwards from the lip of the old shaft. Unable to move further she crouched, staring ahead and waiting for the shaking of her body to ease.

Gradually conscious again of her surroundings, Amy felt cold and rubbed her hands along her arms. She raised her head to draw air deep into her lungs and saw on the far side of the gaping maw, a woman clad in a black coat with a matching hat, angled across her forehead. Silent and unmoving the two women regarded each other. With a cognisant incline of her head, Lucy Tunney disappeared and the morning sun shone warm on Amy.

*   *   *

Red and blue lights flashing, a car with 'Police,' written across its bonnet and along its sides braked in her driveway and a frantic Matt tumbled from the rear seat.

'Amy,' he shouted her name as he ran, circling the gaping maw of the mine shaft with barely a glance. 'Amy, are you alright? Oh sweetheart, what happened?' He knelt beside her and gathered her in his arms. 'Oh God, what . . . .' he caught sight of the gaping hole.

'Keep back sir,' the policeman now out of the car and close behind Matt, placed a restraining hand on his arm as he stood to look down the old mine shaft. 'Let me.' He moved cautiously to the lip of the maw and leaned over to peer down. Hastily he stepped back and moved across to his car to call for backup.

CHAPTER TWENTY-THREE

The retrieval of Max Harrelson's body had been quite an operation. More police turned up with an ambulance minutes behind. The fire brigade arrived with ladders and equipment. Then the delicate retrieval of the body began. Even then no-one was able to tell the actual depth of the mineshaft. It had been capped years ago they said. Its collapse showed a concrete slab wedged sideways far down. It was there they found Max, flung over the ragged edge like a broken puppet, his pale blue eyes staring sightlessly at his rescuers.

White faced, Amy had waited and watched while large trucks with wires and pulleys attached, backed into her yard, and men in overalls and hard hats and carrying big torches, began the process of retrieval. Matt waited beside her, one arm tucking her close to his side while he murmured comforting assurances every now and then.

*   *   *

189

The ambulance with its attendants and Max Harrelson's body had departed followed by rescuers, their trucks and equipment, then the police, the last to leave. Iron guards had been placed around the yawning hole in the centre of Amy's back yard.

'Sit here.' Matt deposited Amy on a kitchen chair with the care of one handling the most delicate of porcelain. He busied himself with cups, hot tea and sugar, then placed two small white pills on the table before Amy.

'No,' she shook her head, 'I'm not taking them.'

'Amy, you must. The doctor left them for you.' Matt crouched in front of her.

'No, I'm fine Matt, really.'

'Your hands are shaking,' he pointed out. 'Reaction is beginning to set in.'

She looked into his eyes and saw only love and concern for her. 'Just for you then.' She bent forward and kissed the tip of his nose then swallowed the tablets.

*   *   *

There was not a lot of officialdom to be coped with concerning Max Harrelson's death. The mineshaft was examined and the conclusion as to the cause of the cave-in was put down to the length of time since it was last capped and the material used not first class.

190

The recent telephone call from the police in Brisbane concerning Amy's safety, and a copy of Max's record had cleared everything up with little fuss and as little stress for her as could be managed. She was now free to once again begin the process of getting on with her life.

From time to time Amy thought of when she had looked into the eyes of Lucy Tunney standing on the opposite side of the mineshaft, and of the message she saw in them.

*   *   *

The inquest concerning Georgie Tunney had been held. Christmas and New Year was past, and the countryside was brown and yellow with the long settled heat of summer.

It was stiflingly hot as the small group stood clustered together at the cemetery watching as the tiny white coffin holding the remains of little George Arthur Tunney was placed in the grave to rest with his grandparents. The last blessing was said and everyone turned to retrace their steps to the cemetery gates.

'Are you going to do anything about Gladys?' Libby asked. She adjusted her wide brimmed hat to shield her face from the sun, the bright gleam of her wedding ring flashing in the strong light.

'No.' Amy shook her head. 'I . . . we,' she corrected herself, 'thought we'd just have a piece added on to Georgie's plaque. "Loved son of Gladys." Something like that.'

'Poor little boy.' Libby brushed at her eyes.

'I think they'll be at peace now, all of them,' Amy said as they reached the cemetery gates. She exchanged hugs with Libby and Jim then got into the car and turned to smile at Matt as he climbed into the driver's seat.

'Okay?' He grinned at her.

'Okay,' she sighed and settled back, one finger rubbing lightly over the ruby and diamond ring on her left hand as he started the engine and drove off.

*   *   *

If Amy from time to time relived the moments when she had looked into the eyes of Lucy Tunney the day Max died, she kept it to herself. One day she would tell Matt about it, but not yet. Not yet.

Chivers Large Print Direct

If you have enjoyed this Large Print book and would like to build up your own collection of Large Print books and have them delivered direct to your door, please contact **Chivers Large Print Direct**.

Chivers Large Print Direct offers you a full service:

☆ **Created to support your local library**

☆ **Delivery direct to your door**

☆ **Easy-to-read type and attractively bound**

☆ **The very best authors**

☆ **Special low prices**

For further details either call Customer Services on 01225 443400 or write to us at

Chivers Large Print Direct
FREEPOST (BA 1686/1)
Bath
BA1 3QZ